BRAVE LIKE LILY

RICHARD CARDENAS

1

BRAVE LIKE LILY

Copyright © 2019 by Richard Cardenas

ISBN: 978-1070988856

Printed and bound in the U.S.A.

I'D LIKE TO DEDICATE THIS BOOK TO THE VICTIMS AND FAMILIES AFFECTED BY POLICE BRUTALITY AND SOCIAL INJUSTICE. MAY THIS INSPIRE YOU, THE READER, TO SPEAK UP AND HAVE A VOICE. BRAVERY LIVES INSIDE ALL OF US. FIND IT. USE IT. - R.C.

My sister Lily is in a box now. I hate the color of the casket and I know Lily would've hated it too. In fact, if she were still alive, she would've written one of her awesome short stories on why the color pink disgusted her beyond belief. I sigh and cross my arms. But she isn't alive anymore. She's in a freaking box and right this second she is being lowered into the ground with a machine that is making an incredibly annoying sound.

Probably sensing what I'm about to do, my mom latches a hand onto my shoulder and pinches it. I halt my next move and wait for her to unlatch her grip on me. She's afraid I'm going to do something stupid, because I always do something stupid. It's not just how she feels. It's how my parents feel, it's how my other sister Nina feels, and it's how my aunt Terry feels.

But it isn't how abuelo Mango feels, it's not how

my best friend Queenie feels, and it's not how I feel. I just have a lot of emotions and unlike everybody else, I don't have a key to the box that they are supposed to stay inside of. So they come out whenever they want to.

My specialty is breaking things. Like this morning, I kicked a hole through my bedroom door and scraped my leg pretty bad. Nina called me a weirdo and then went back to curling her hair.

I have IED (Intermittent Explosive Disorder), it's something a lot of doctors and people don't believe in, but it's real. People often confuse it with Bipolar Disorder and it gets annoying when I have to explain it over and over. With IED I get real angry, real quick and have an outburst, or tantrum, or episode. It always ends in me breaking something or hurting someone, though I haven't hurt anyone since I was nine when I punched my uncle Manny in the mouth. Some people cry, some people verbally attack, but I tend to scream, really loud and it is non-stop when I have a bad outburst.

I usually take medication for it, but the kind the last doctor gave me turned me into the walking dead. I couldn't do anything but sit and stare. So my mom and dad took me off of it, which is a good thing and a bad thing. *The good thing?* I don't act like the undead. *The bad thing?* The outbursts. But for right now we deal with it, as a family, the best way we can.

I can feel my mom's nails dig into my skin and I bite down on my bottom lip. I know she's not doing it to be mean, she's scared. But I just want to make sure they don't drop Lily inside the pit like she doesn't mean anything anymore, like she's just an empty sack of skin and bones.

When my mom finally lets go, I hurry away from her side and walk over to my dad, positioning myself so that I can't see the worrisome glare from my mom.

"Do you want to go get a smoothie after this?" My dad sits his hand on top of my head, something he knows I hate, and smiles at me. I just turned thirteen and he still treats me like I'm nine. Lily is nineteen, or *was* nineteen. I swallow hard.

"Lily hated smoothies," I say, chewing on my entire bottom lip, something I knew well enough my mom hates.

The smile falls from my dad's face and he looks over at the pit. I didn't mean to hurt his feelings. I want to my punch myself. I always say the wrong things.

"Yes, she did, didn't she?" I notice that his eyes are red and swollen. I look around and notice that everyone else's eyes are the same, especially my mom's. Her eyes are so swollen that you can't even see the color of them, which is brown, just like Lily's.

Frustration rises inside of me. Why aren't my eyes red and swollen? Why haven't I cried yet? The frustration quickly turns into guilt and just as quickly the guilt turns into disgust and I want to hit something. I tear myself away from my dad's hand and walk over to the pit.

"Mijo, come away from there!" My mom's whisper itches my ear like an annoying fly. But I don't listen. I just stand here watching as my older sister's casket meets the bottom of the pit. I can hear the wood of the casket settle and for a second I wonder if Lily has come back to life. Maybe she's trying to call out my name, or she's trying to claw at the inside of the lid?

But then I remember that this is real life and stuff like that just doesn't happen.

I reach into my coat pocket and retrieve a dried maple leaf from Lily's room, luckily it hasn't fallen apart. This particular leaf was her favorite one because I found it for her when I was younger. She had it pinned to her bedroom wall ever since, along with the rest of her leaf collection.

I know my mom and dad can see what's in my hand and I know they are both angry because I went into Lily's room and took it without asking. But no one would let me put something inside her casket and she would've wanted this leaf with her because it was her favorite thing in the world. She needs it, like I still need her.

With a flick of my wrist, I toss the leaf into the pit and it feels like a bowling ball has dropped onto my chest.

I hear the whispering clatter of it landing on the casket's lid and my arms start to tingle with anger. How is she going to get it if it's outside of her casket? What if it gets smashed by all the dirt?

"Damn it!" I yell and turn around to see my mom heading directly toward me. She thinks I'm going to do something, but I'm not. At least I don't think I am. She has her arms open, ready to capture me like a loving Venus flytrap.

I scoot away from Lily's grave. Oddly enough just a few feet away from Lily's grave site is a giant tree I used to climb on when me and Lily would come to this cemetery to look for leaves. I remember climbing to the top and being able to stare over the entire cemetery, it's that high. Without really giving it a second thought, I start climbing up the tree until I'm high enough to not be snatched by my mom's hands.

"Mijo, come down from there this instant. You're embarrassing this family," my mom says in a voice I know all too well. It's the voice that means business and a chancla if I don't obey. So I start climbing back down and shake my hair down over my eyes so I can't see if anyone looks at me.

A chunk of my suit gets caught on a branch and

frustratingly I yank it off and realize too late that it wasn't the smartest thing to do. I turn just in time to see that I'm falling straight down onto the ground below. As if I don't ruin things enough.

I broke my stupid leg. I can't think of anything more horrifying and embarrassing at the same time. After trying so hard that entire morning to not do anything stupid, I failed, just like I always do. Fortunately, as my abuelo Mango said, no one was even looking at me when I fell. I guess that's a good thing.

My mom and dad and Nina still aren't saying much to me. Nina says I did it for attention, Dad says I need to go back on medication, and my mom says it was just an accident. Abuelo Mango says that I'm just sad and that I shouldn't let what everyone else is saying get to me. He said sadness is like a pit and that I've already fallen down inside and now I just need to find a way out.

Unlike everyone else, abuelo Mango gets me. But then again, sometimes abuelo Mango thinks my name is Benito and that we are still in 1958.

Rain attacks my bedroom window like tiny pebbles being thrown by the neighborhood bully Jesse Martinez. He's probably already told everyone at school that I fell out of a tree at my sister's funeral. He's a jackass, or so my uncle Paco says. I toss a wad of warm popcorn at the window. The popcorn lands on the hardwood and Coco, Lily's cat, leaps off of my bed and starts to nibble on the popcorn. I swear that cat will eat anything.

Two weeks ago Lily was shot by a police officer. A *white one*, my dad said and got real angry when he said it the other night at dinner. I used to think they only shot black people like that, Nina said after Dad spoke. Mom silenced her with a glare and the rest of dinner was silent as church on a Sunday afternoon.

But it's all over the local news. Helena Flores on KOSX news said that what happened was tragic and that hopefully justice will be served. After she said that they let people call in and voice their opinions and a man called in and said that "Mexicans" and "African-Americans" are the core of violence in the U.S. and that the police officer shouldn't be blamed.

Blame. That's the word of the year, I think. You either blame the police officer who killed my sister or you blame my sister for being out at 3am with her friends ghost hunting at the cemetery. Most people blame the police officer, who had only been on the streets for two months. But I don't know who to blame yet and it's starting to bother me too much.

It makes a pain in my chest, as if someone is holding my heart with their hand and squeezing when I try to breathe.

My dad says that I'm just too young to get it, but that I should be blaming the officer and the crappy justice system. My uncle Paco says that if he knew the police officer's name, he'd hurt him back real bad. I hope he never learns his name.

My family found out two days after Lily died that the reason the officer shot Lily, was because he thought she was pulling a gun out of her jacket. It wasn't a gun. It was an inhaler. The detective that was sitting in Lily's chair at the dinner table said that Lily and her friends were running from the police officer and that if they hadn't run off, none of this would've happened. My dad told the detective to leave.

An investigation has already started but my uncle Paco thinks the officer won't get in trouble for anything. My mom and dad keep themselves updated by our civil rights lawyer Devon Curtis. My aunt told us to contact him after what happened to Lily that night.

All of this hurts, but not enough to make me cry. Trust me, I'm really mad at myself for not crying. Even Queenie, my best friend, cried at the funeral and she was close with Lily, too. Lily was the one who taught Queenie how to run a protest and how to roller skate when she was eight. I just don't get why I haven't cried yet.

Queenie says that the tears will come in time. I don't know why I can't cry. I've cried before, like when we had to put our dog Rocky to sleep a couple of years ago. I cried so hard that I couldn't see for two days because of how puffy my eyes were. Now, I'm scared to cry. I hate myself.

At least that's not the only thing I have to worry about. I'm going back to school in the morning in a freaking wheelchair with a sister who is dead and never coming back.

Whenever I felt real bad, Rocky was always there. He was there for me after an outburst, he was there for me when I was sad another boy didn't like me back, he was everything to me. Rocky was a white pitbull with a gray patch over his left eye and he was my best friend. He supposedly belonged to my dad, but did my dad pick up his poop and train him to pee on puppy pads? It was all me. So I always considered Rocky mine. He loved Lily just as much as me so I guess he belonged to her too.

Rocky had a thing for tearing things up. He couldn't help but take one of Nina's favorite shoes and turn it into a work of mangled Rocky art. Just like with me, I can't help if I get so angry at times that I destroy something or hurt myself in the process. It's just a part of who we are. I just realized that I compared myself to a dog. I guess I'm more messed up than I thought.

Lily and I used to take him on walks after he tore something up. It would calm him down and when we'd get back, he'd be too tired to search for something to demolish. My mom praised us for our discovery.

It ended up becoming routine and after Rocky got cancer and had to be put down, it was hard for me to change this routine. I'd jump up from my bed, run over and snatch his leash off the wall hook by the garage and then it would hit me. He wasn't there anymore. I did this for a few days. I'd stand there at the back door with his red leash in my hands and just cry. And then a couple of days later on a Friday afternoon, I noticed that his leash had disappeared.

That exact moment set me off. I shattered the back sliding door with several slams of my fist and couldn't stop screaming. The next thing I knew, Lily was cradling me in her arms and combing her hand through my hair.

"It's alright, Dumbo." Lily was holding onto me tightly because she knew if she let go, I'd cause more damage to the house. I kept screaming into her chest and then I started crying. We sat there for a while on the kitchen floor, Lily holding me and singing her favorite song over and over.

The rest of the house was empty. Mom and Dad were visiting abuelo Mango at Aunt Terry's house and Nina was with her boyfriend. It was just Lily and me.

"I'm sorry," I told her as I began to calm down.

"What have I told you time and time again?" Lily said to me.

"You don't have to be sorry for something you can't control," I told her, keeping my head against her chest. I was still a little shaky but I was fine. I looked down at my hand and miraculously I'd only had a few scrapes. I was expecting to have sliced my hand open, but this time I was pretty lucky.

"Hey, you wanna go take a walk around the park?" Lily pulled me away from her chest and looked at me. I didn't like anyone to look at me after an outburst, but I always let Lily, because Lily didn't look at me with pity or anger, she looked at me with love and her awesome, contagious smile.

"But we only went walking with Rocky," I said, feeling sad all over again. I missed him so much that it hurt to even think of him sometimes.

"Well, we can walk *for* him, okay Dumbo?"Lily smiled and flicked both of my ears.

I let Lily pull me up from the floor. Ever since, right after an outburst, Lily and I would go for a walk. Nina had told Lily that I wasn't a dog. But it wasn't about that. We had something we'd done for Rocky that worked and interestingly enough it somehow worked for me too. Mom and Dad didn't mind it at all.

I didn't care what Nina thought, Lily didn't either. It helped me calm down and it gave Lily and I more time to hang out together. I'm not sure if I could do it on my own now. It just wouldn't feel right. But I guess that is just something I'll have to find out. The walking did remind me of Rocky a lot, but in a good way, and Lily would tell me that Rocky was always with us, we just couldn't see him, like the wind.

"Come on, Dumbo!" Lily said, grabbing a cherry

Pepsi from the fridge, her favorite drink. Lily called me Dumbo because my ears were big. Of course, she knew I hated it. But it was *our* thing. It will always be our thing.

I hate waking up at 6:30am, especially on a Monday morning. I hate waking up for now because when I wake up, I think things are the same. I think, Lily's probably hogging the hallway bathroom so I'll have to use Mom and Dad's to pee. When it hits me that I can pee in the hallway bathroom, I start to get angry. The urge to kick something begins but then I remember I'm in a wheelchair and I can't really kick anything.

My mom has to dress me now, which I hate, because I have hair down there now and I don't want her to see it. She makes it a point not to stare down there when she changes my underwear. But she does make it a point to tell me that I'm too old for Batman boxers.

I tell her that no one is too old for Batman boxers.

"But you need new chones, mijo. You're thirteen now. I'll go buy some today after I drop off Lily's..." my mom's voice disappears, lost somewhere in my room. Quickly, she gets up from squatting, tells me that she forgot the stove was on and leaves my room.

Not a second later, Nina pops her head into my room and shakes it.

"Why did you make her cry, you little turd?" she snaps at me.

"I didn't make her cry, stupida!"

"Mom, Mateo is cussing!" Nina smirks at me.

"MATEO!" my mom yells from the kitchen.

"You're such a pain, Mateo," she says then leaves my doorway. Nina says my name weird, like Mat-tay-yo. She's been doing it for the past couple of years ever since she met her boyfriend Gage. Lily says, or *used* to say, that Nina likes to think she's white. Just let her think she's Emma Stone, Lily used to say. One day she'll see how crazy she is and go back to acting like Selena like the rest of us, Lily said that too. Lily said a lot of things, things I miss very badly.

The house feels different without her. It feels like when one speaker goes out in a car. It's a big fat silence and you notice it and you want to do something about it, but you can't. Sometimes it's too much and I have to put on the TV and watch something to get my mind off of it. Lily hated the TV. She liked nature and books more.

"Mateo, you're going to be late!" my dad charges into my bedroom and begins pushing me out of the room by the handles on my wheelchair.

"I can do it, Dad!" I snap, not meaning to, and wheel myself down the hallway. When I notice that I'm about to pass Lily's room, I stop and stare at her closed bedroom door. The pain begins again, as if it were on pause, waiting for something to press play. I haven't been inside her room since the morning of her funeral and I didn't even have my eyes fully open, I just walked in, grabbed the leaf and ran out.

"Move it, dummy." Nina shoves my wheelchair with her hip and blocks my sight of Lily's door. Before I can talk myself out of doing what I'm about to do, I push my chair forward and run over Nina's foot.

In the van, my dad is driving pretty fast. My uncle Paco made a little stand so I can put my cast on it while I'm in the van. I didn't expect it to help, but it does. Paco is my dad's little brother. They hate each other and love each other at the same time. Paco was my abuela Lulu's favorite, even though he can't keep a job to save his life and has five kids that he doesn't take care of, via my mom's weekly phone gossip.

My dad is angry because I ran over Nina's foot and she had to limp out to Gage's car for her ride to school. My dad hates Gage and doesn't want Nina in his car because she's only sixteen but the thing about Nina is that she tends to get whatever she wants.

"You need to chill yourself out, Mateo. Taking your anger out on your sister is not how you handle your IED. Dr. Montoya told you that when you feel an outburst or an anger spur coming, you count to thirteen and try to regulate your breathing. Unless you want to go back on those meds that turned you into a zombie, you'll try. Right, you'll try?" I don't have to look up to know that my dad is staring at me from the rear-view mirror. But I know that I have to look, because when he talks to you, you look at him. So I look and instantly regret it. He looks disappointed in me.

"Yes," I say. "I'll try." I'd never get put back on those meds no matter what I do. My mom said that I'm not myself when I'm on them and I agree, but my dad just wants me to be better. Sometimes he thinks I need them. But the thing with moms is that even if dads think they're in charge, they really aren't.

"Good." My dad says and even though he doesn't want to, he lets a tiny smile creep onto his face. That's how I know he still loves me. Because it's not a smile that says "damn, right" or "you better" it's a "This kid is something else, but I love him." smile, or at least that's what I get from it.

"I miss Lily," I say aloud, even though I didn't mean to. My face gets hot and red. Sometimes I say things out loud I mean to say in my head. This is a problem, and sometimes, a big one.

My dad pulls into my school's parking lot and turns off the engine. He stares at the steering wheel for what feels like forever. The wrinkles on his face form a map of sadness and I want to smooth it all out and tell him I'm sorry for making him sad. I tend to be sorry a lot.

Finally, he looks into the rear-view mirror and smiles at me. His eyes are red. Lately, they're always red.

"Me, too, mijo. *Me too.*"

I'm early, *too* early for school. Before I left the house my mom told me not to talk to anyone other than Queenie. She told me I had to wait in the office for her or Dad to pick me up after school. She told me not to talk to the media, but I already knew that. Instead of trying to do something about what happened, they'd rather ask stupid questions like:

Was Lily a devil worshiper? Did Lily have bad grades? Did Lily own a gun or a knife? How come Lily was in a cemetery at 3am? Why did she run? Why didn't she just let herself get caught?

Just thinking of the questions gets me mad, so I quickly wheel myself toward the cafeteria to eat something. I can calm down if I eat something. I can count the grapes on the tray or the oats in the oatmeal and it will help. It always does.

When I wheel myself through the doors, two of the lunch ladies see me and slam their hands over their chests. One of them is a friend of my mom's from church, Crystal. I wheel myself over to the non-existent breakfast line and punch in my number.

"Pobrecito, what happened?" Crystal asks.

"I fell out of a tree," I say but I feel like they already know.

Crystal giggles and then almost instantly she stops. It doesn't take me long to recognize what she's thinking of.

"I'm so sorry about Lily, mijito. She was such a sweet and beautiful girl." Crystal smiles down at me and I guess feeling bad for me, she adds a third dollop of oatmeal and grapes onto my tray.

"Gracias," is all I have for her. Instead of looking at their sad, chubby, faces, I take my tray and wheel myself over to a vacant table. I can see the janitor from the corner of my eye but I don't look at him. I don't want to see the look on his face, because I already know it's a sad one.

I look down at my oatmeal and begin to count the oats. In less than ten minutes I've counted over a sixty oats and now my stupid oatmeal is cold.

I didn't notice that people were coming into the cafeteria while I was counting oats. There are four guys across the way from me in a booth but they aren't even paying attention to me, which I like. One of them is Marcus Brooks. Ever since last year I've thought he was cute. As if he can hear the thoughts inside of my head, he turns to me.

I freeze like a deer in headlights and instead of looking at me weird or cussing me out for staring at him, he smiles. I smile back. But then our smiling contest is cut short by the appearance of Dakota Hanes, Marcus's ex-girlfriend. Now he's staring at her as she scoots into the booth next to him and lays her head on his shoulder. He shakes her head off and she swats him on the chest.

Then as if being smacked in the face, a thought pops into my head. How in the heck can you be interested in a boy after your sister has just died? The thought makes me feel guilty and sick, so I look back down at my tray and start shoveling the oatmeal into my mouth like a zoo animal.

After I've scarfed down my breakfast, I take the tray and wheel myself over to the trash bin. That's when I notice the silence that has taken over the cafeteria. It's as if someone has hit *mute* on a remote control. I can almost hear my heart beat.

I look away from the trash bin and see fifty or so of my fellow students staring directly at me. One girl mouths that she's sorry and one boy smiles and then looks back down at his tray. This is the moment I've dreaded so much on the ride from home to here. I start to get nervous and back into the trash bin by accident.

"What are you all staring at? Eat your breakfast before it gets cold!" a voice comes from behind me and I don't have to turn my chair to know that it's Queenie, but I do anyway. There standing in the doorway of the cafeteria, with one hand on her hip, and the other cradling her beloved purple rhinestone iPad, is my best friend since kindergarten, Queenie Sutton.

Queenie winks at me and then fixes her hazel eyes on the students behind me. The thing about Queenie is that she's kind of amazing and when Queenie talks, you listen. Almost instantly, the ruckus of the cafeteria revives and everyone is back to normal, except for me.

"Come on, I have something to show you," Queenie says and turns to walk back out of the cafeteria, her lavender colored braids swinging. Before I leave, I turn my chair back around to see if I can find Marcus, but he's not there anymore. Dakota glares at me for some reason, as if she knows why I'm looking over there and then almost as quickly as I spun myself around, I bolt from the cafeteria as if the wheels of my chair are on fire.

Queenie is walking so fast that I'm burning the palms of my hands on my wheels trying to keep up with her. The last time I saw Queenie was at Lily's funeral. As we hurry through the 100 hall as if we're being chased, Queenie realizes just how fast she's going and stops. I catch up to her and she puts a hand on a handle of my chair and smiles down at me.

"Why did you pick yellow?" Queenie is staring at the cast on my right leg.

"It's Lily's favorite color." I tell her. There I go again, saying things I mean to say in my head. I look at her to see if I've struck something, to see if she looks hurt or wants to cry. But instead she pulls out a sharpie from her shoulder bag and squats down to my level.

"Lily would've liked it," Queenie says and starts drawing something on my cast. I don't know what my mom and dad will think. They told me not to let anyone write stupid stuff on it, but this is Queenie and Queenie's not just anyone.

I wait for her to move her hand and see that she's drawn a maple leaf. I stare at her drawing, though it's not completely perfect, it's a maple leaf. Queenie knew about Lily's love for leaves and anything to do with nature, so it seems only fitting that she'd draw a leaf.

"I drew one just like this on her binder last summer." Queenie's eyes are filling with tears and she wipes them away with the sleeve of her jacket. "Now, follow me!"

We're halfway down the 200 hall when I spot a giant white poster on a wall. It's a poster I've never seen before. It's a poster with Lily's face on it.

Queenie stops in front of it and gestures to it, as if it is something to be excited about.

In the middle of the poster is the photo the news has been using for what happened to Lily. It was taken at Yosemite National Park last year. We had a lot of fun those couple of days we were there. Lily was so happy because of all the trees and all the different plants she could look at and take pictures of. It was one of the best summers ever. And now we'll never have any summers like that ever again.

I pull myself back to the present. I'm still staring at the poster. On the bottom of Lily's photo is a hashtag in giant black bold font: **#JusticeForLilyMorales**. On the bottom of that is a time and date for a candlelight vigil that will take place on October 25th, in front of the library on Stevens street. It's right across from the police department too.

My chest is hurting and my head is throbbing.

"I got them made yesterday. I got here early and put them all over the school," Queenie sounds really happy with herself. The anger in me is at the surface and instead of trying to press it back down, I let it out.

"Why didn't you ask me if I was okay with this?" I turn to her. I'm gripping the sides of my chair. Her face morphs from a happy smile to a frown. She knows about my outbursts and even though I've only ever had two that she's actually witnessed, she can already tell this is turning into one.

"I didn't think you'd mind, Mateo." Queenie begins twisting her fingers.

"MY SISTER'S FACE IS ALL OVER THE SCHOOL." My tonsils rattle. My voice is loud, too loud. Calm down, I tell myself. You can do this on your own, I tell myself. I grip the sides of my chair tighter and count to thirteen. I count again, and again. What feels like forever, my chest stops heaving and my head isn't throbbing anymore. My teeth hurt from grinding them so hard.

Queenie is still standing there, waiting.

"I'm sorry," I tell her, not looking directly at her face, because I can't. I feel guilty for yelling at her. I'm embarrassed.

"It's okay, Mateo. It's okay." Queenie tells me and I finally look at her. She's not scared or angry at me. "But don't you want justice for your sister?"

I look over at the poster and stare into my sister's face.

"I do but I don't know how," I say.

"What do you mean, you don't know how?" Queenie turns to me and crosses her arms. "Your sister was just killed by a police officer because he thought her inhaler was a gun and so far he's not getting punished for it, Mateo. My dad says that's wrong and so do I... *do you?*"

I tear my eyes away from Lily's face and look into Queenie's. She has her arms crossed, defiant as usual. I haven't told her how I feel about everything, the blaming, the whole justice thing. I don't feel like I fully understand it.

"Of course I think it's wrong. But I just don't know how to feel, Queenie." Here, I go. "I'm mad, I'm sad, and I want to know why she had to die and why she had to die like that. But I don't know how to want justice for my sister? I don't know how to blame a man for killing my sister. I just don't freaking know!"

Queenie squats down to my level and stares right into my eyes.

"You're confused and I get that, Mateo. Do you remember when Francine Baker got killed by those police officers last spring? Lily helped me start that little protest I put together. She shouldn't be forgotten like Francine was."

The thing is I do want my sister to be remembered. I do want the news to keep talking about her. I do want to understand why that officer shot my sister and how he could do something like that to someone like Lily, someone who lit up a room with her smile and jokes. Someone who inspired people like Queenie. I feel useless. I feel guilty. I feel horrible.

"I'm just not good at all this stuff."

"That's why I'm helping you. I'm doing this for you, for Lily, and for all the other people who lost their lives to this stupid broken system." Queenie smiles up at the poster. "We're going to get justice, Mateo."

The bell rings, letting me know it's time to face

my first class of the day. More sad faces to avoid, more sorrys for me to hear, more stares.

"Don't worry, I got you. See you at lunch." Queenie smiles at me and takes off down the hall. People are already bustling into the hall around me. I can hear the skids of shoes on the ground and whispers floating in the air. To avoid it all, I look back up at the poster and stare at my sister's smiling face.

I'm the last one to get to Mrs. Harper's class.
When she sees me roll in, she puts her jumbo dry-erase
marker down and turns to me. Everyone else is staring,
but I'm doing my best to avoid all of their eyes. I run
over someone's backpack and whisper sorry at them.
There's nowhere for me to park my chair and I'm
starting to get nervous.

"Mr. Morales," Mrs. Harper calls my name and I
spin in the chair toward her, knocking someone's
binder to the ground. She has both of her long hands
wrapped around her torso, like she's hugging herself.
This is different. I've never seen her like this before.
She looks like she feels bad for me, which is new to me.
She's not usually very nice to me, or anyone else.

"Yes, Mrs. Harper," I say, rolling toward her. I
stop next to her desk and she crosses her arms this
time. She knocks her blonde bangs out of her vision

and points to the classroom door.

"You are to report to the assistant principal's office immediately." She sounds different too. She's not commanding me like I did something bad, her voice is soft and kind.

Instead of asking why, I just say okay and hurry out of the classroom, bumping into the sides of the doorway on the way out.

Ten minutes later I'm sitting in the assistant principal's office. It smells like peppermint gum and lemon air freshener. I hate both of those scents. The tiny silver plaque stuck to a large brown desk reads: Mrs. Oberlin. I've never met her before, but I've seen her around. She seems nice. But that's how I felt the first time I met Mrs. Harper and she turned out to be pretty evil, except for today.

The door opens and I sit up straight as if I'm about to be scolded. A woman, skinny as a pencil walks into the room and sits down at her desk without looking at me. She pulls a folder out from a drawer, looks it over and then puts it down in front of her. I watch as she pumps a few globs of anti-bacterial gel into her hands and massages it into her skin. It's almost as if I'm a ghost.

As if sensing my thoughts, she tilts her head up and stares directly at me. Her eyes are blue, shockingly blue, and her lips are as red as blood.

"Hi, Mr. Morales, I'm Mrs. Oberlin. Now, don't be nervous, you're not in any sort of trouble. We, Mr. Winslow and I, think it would be best, under the recent set of circumstances, that you should be omitted from attending any of your regular classes for the remainder of the month." She's smiling, a giant weird smile at me and it kind of makes me uncomfortable.

I didn't want to come to school and now the school doesn't want me to, so I guess I got what I wanted. I wonder how Mom and Dad are going to handle this. I'd rather be home anyway than wheeling myself around school having people stare at me for the rest of the month or however long they feel like it.

"So is my mom coming to pick me up?" I ask.

Mrs. Oberlin lets a laugh escape through her scary smile.

"Oh no, you see we don't want to send you home. We've arranged for you to be in the school library for the rest of the month. Mrs. York is excited to have some help and to have you in there for a while. We'll see about getting your school work to you, but mostly we just want you to be... how do I put this... um... safe, yes, safe."

Safe? What the heck does that even mean? Not wanting to talk about any of this even more, I nod and say okay.

"Wonderful. We'll have a chat with your parents about this and if you need anything, Mr. Morales, you come straight to my office." The scary smile is back.

"Thanks, I guess." I say and watch her as she hands me a lamented card connected to a black and orange lanyard. It looks like my school ID, but when I turn it over I see a tiny paragraph and a signature of the principal and Mrs. Oberlin:

Mateo Morales is to be in the school library at ALL TIMES, including lunch, and after school until he is picked up by a parent/guardian. If seen outside of library during school hours, please return him to the library and Mrs. York.

Sincerely,
Albert Winslow & Claire Oberlin

I read the card over and over.

Return? Like I'm some kind of stupid lost sweater.

I know why they want me inside of the library. It took me a few minutes to put the pieces together but I know now. They want me in here so I don't cause trouble for the school, so I don't break something, so I don't hurt someone. They aren't thinking about my safety. They're thinking about their safety.

But what the heck do they think I'm going to do? I'm in a wheelchair for a while. I'm trying to think of what my dad will say. I don't know if he'll be angry with me for having a reputation, or angry at the school for putting me away like a disobedient dog. I guess I'll find out when I get home.

I'm sitting at a table pulled to the side specifically for me. How do I know this? There's a lime green piece of construction paper taped to the top of the table that reads: Reserved for Mateo Morales. And there's no chair.

I'm pretty familiar with the library. I don't read much, but Lily read a lot. I remember when she made me read the first Magnus Chase book because she needed to talk to someone about it. I should read more.

To take my mind off everything I look around the library while sitting behind my table. There's no one else in here, not even Mrs. York. I've only ever met Mrs. York when we came in here for classes, which is twice. I know she's kinda nice and she's married to Natasha York, the volleyball coach, but that's pretty much it.

I swear people can tell when I'm thinking about them because just as I'm thinking of Mrs. York, the doors to the library hiss open and in comes in this tall woman in a charcoal gray suit and red heels. But she isn't Mrs. York. Mrs. York is black and this lady is white. She turns my way, smiles, and that's when I see that she has a device in her hand.

She's with the news or something and even though I've been tucked away inside of the library, she's found me.

"Mateo Morales?" She asks.

Should I lie? Should I tell her to leave me alone? I don't know what to do and now my chest is hurting again. I'm not good with confrontation. I don't want to be here. I just want to go home. I ... I... I look up and into her face and fold my hands on top of the table, *defiant*, like Queenie.

"What do you want?" I tell her.

She takes that as an invitation and drags a chair over to my table and sits down across from me. She smells like burnt coffee.

"I'd like to speak to you about what happened to your sister. I'm here to get the truth. I'm not here to hurt your feelings, Mateo." She says my name like Nina does.

I try to scoot up in my chair, but this stupid cast is weighing my leg down. I'm trying to seem like my uncle Paco, tough. I probably look like an idiot or like I have to go take a gigantic dump.

"I'm not supposed to talk to people like you," I tell her.

"I understand that, but it would help if I got just a simple quote from you. It could help a lot. Wouldn't you like to help?"

I look at her face and she seems different now that she's sitting down with me. She reminds me of the wolf in Red Riding Hood. Evil and sneaky.

"I'm sorry," I tell her, obeying my mom and dad. "I can't talk to you."

She clears her throat and presses a button on the device in her hand. She's going to try and talk to me anyway. In this moment, she's the wolf and I'm Red Riding Hood.

"Did your sister hang out with the wrong crowd?" she asks. I can see little chips of red lipstick on her front teeth, or fangs.

I sit in silence and it feels like an hour has gone

by, but the bell hasn't rung and Mrs. York still isn't here. And this lady isn't leaving.

"Why was your sister going to pull a gun on the officer who shot her?"

For as long as I am sitting here, I think of how strong I am to not give into this lady, to not give into the wolf. But I can't help but realize that something inside of me has snapped, like a twig. I'm going to open my mouth and there's nothing I can do to stop it. Mom, Dad, I'm sorry.

"My sister didn't have a gun. She had asthma. She was trying to get to her inhaler." I explain to her.

"Well, my sources tell me that she was involved with Pete Morales's crew. Isn't that your uncle? Did you know your uncle is the head of a local gang? Was your sister a part of it too?"

I'm getting really angry and I can't stop it.

"What does that have to do with her being killed?"

"Excuse me?" Out of the corner of my eye I see a woman in the library's doorway. The wolf quickly gets up from the table and winks at me, *sneaky*.

"Nice speaking with you, Mateo." She tells me and walks passed the woman I now recognize as Mrs. York. Mrs. York grabs the woman by her gray blazer and stops her in her tracks.

"You know damn well you're not allowed on school premises. Now, get the hell out of here before I call school security." Mrs. York lets go of the woman's clothes and the wolf rushes out of the library with a smirk on her face, *evil*.

Mrs. York turns to me, running a hand through her short fro. Her hands are shaking and her coffee is spilling out of the cup in her hand. I can see the steam rising out of the cup and wonder how hot it must feel running down her hand. But it's like she doesn't even notice it.

"They said you wouldn't be sent here until after lunch. I'm so sorry, Mr. Morales. This was not how it was supposed to go. Crap, they're going to blame me and have my head for this." She's talking to herself now, whispering to the air.

I feel bad for her. She didn't know I'd be in here and she surely didn't think a person from the media would sneak into the school to find me. Her hands are still shaking and I know how that feels. She's nervous. So I decide to help her.

"If they ask what happened, I'll tell them that lady caught me outside in the quad." Mrs. York turns to me, her eyes large and watery.

"I can't ask you to do that, Mr. Morales." She wipes her eyes.

"You're not asking me, I'm offering. Please, Mrs. York, this is not your fault. You're not the one to blame." There it is again, that word, *blame*.

She turns back to me and finally tosses her coffee in the trash since the cup is practically empty. Her eyes are not watery anymore either. She's relieved.

"Okay then." She looks at her hand that the coffee was spilling on and shakes her head. "Looks like I'm going to need an ice pack and more coffee. Would you like a cup?"

I don't say anything, I just nod.

I'm sitting across my table from Mrs. York with a
cup of cold coffee in front of me. She tells me that she's
sorry for what happened with the wolf and she's sorry
for what happened to my sister. She says she knew Lily
and Lily was the only one who joined the library's book
club. They read books together and discussed them
afterward with donuts from Benny's and coffee. That
sounds exactly like Lily to me.

This whole time I've just been sitting and
listening to her. A part of me wants to talk to her, but
another part of me feels like I have nothing to say
because I feel so sad. It's like I'm fighting with myself
on the inside. It sucks.

Mrs. York sees that I'm not really in the talking
mood and tells me she's going to start checking in
books and that afterward she'll teach me how to shelve
them. I nod and she leaves me alone with my cold

coffee.

I pull my phone from my backpack and text Queenie:

ME: They put me in the library for the rest of the month. I won't be at lunch. I'll be in here with Mrs. York.

QUEENIE: WTH!

ME: I'll tell you everything at lunch. Come to the library.

QUEENIE: K, C U then.

I don't know why I do it, but I start going through the pictures on my phone. The first photo is of me and Lily. It's with that stupid dog face filter and we both look funny. The next one is one of Lily sitting in the living room reading. The next one after that is of Lily collecting leaves in the park.

I hear the TV on in Mrs. York's office and when I hear Lily's name, I drop my phone on the table and rush my chair into her office without knocking. She doesn't notice me until the door squeaks and she reaches up to turn her TV off.

"No, don't." I tell her. She listens and brings her hand back down.

The TV reporter is a white man with thinning brown hair and he's talking about my sister like she was some kind of evil person.

They put a photo of Lily up and it's one I've seen before. The photo is of Lily flipping off the camera with her tongue out, her finger blurred. It's a photo from Lily's Facebook profile and it's one that Nina took a few months ago when Nina called Lily a nerd for reading instead of being out partying with her friends. Lily put her book down on her lap and flipped off Nina. I saw it, I was there.

Without asking me this time, Mrs. York turns the TV off. In the silence I can hear my heart beating in my ears. *Why are they doing this to my sister?*

"There was a book on her lap in that photo." I

finally speak, my hands gripping the wheels of my chair in frustration. "My sister Nina took that picture of Lily after Nina called her a nerd. I was there in the living room when it happened. We all laughed. Why are they using that picture? To make her look bad? I don't understand."

Mrs. York walks over to her desk and takes a seat on it.

"They want to make it look good for the police department. Unfortunately this is how the media works sometimes, Mr. Morales. They can be amazing at their jobs, but they can also be heartless and conniving. But it doesn't change what really happened. Your sister was a victim and she deserves justice."

Everybody keeps saying that... *Justice.* But even if the police officer gets in trouble for what he did, that still won't bring my sister back. Lily will still be dead. I won't ever hear my sister's laugh again. I won't ever see her reading in the living room again.

"Yeah... justice." I turn and wheel myself out of her office and back to my table. I put my phone back into my bag and sit there and stare at the bookshelves, the bookshelves my sister once took books from, bookshelves she'll never see again.

Two hours have gone by and then the lunch bell rings.

So far today I've learned that the media can be ugly sometimes, Mrs. York can withstand the heat of fresh coffee like a superhero, and how to shelve books by Dewey decimals.

I'm shelving the biography section now. I didn't think it would be this hard shelving books in a wheelchair, but it is. I've dropped ten books already but Mrs. York says she'll pick those ones up. She says I've taken quickly to how the library works, much like my sister did. I hear my phone go off and already know it's Nina. I have designated text-tones for everybody in my family. Nina's is a Mariachi song that I know she hates because it's "too Mexican".

I take my phone out of my bag and open her message:

Nina: *What the hell did you do, Mateo? Mom and Dad told you not to talk to the freaking media. You messed up big time. – N.*

But I didn't say anything the wolf could use. At least I don't think I did. Instead of responding to Nina, I text Queenie to hurry up and eat lunch so she can get in here. I need to talk to someone. I start seeing little sparkles, like when I get too nervous. I don't need this right now. I don't want to freak out right now. But I'm in so much trouble. My dad's going to yell at me. My mom's going to cry at me. Nina's going to shake her head at me.

"Mateo, aren't you going to eat your lunch?" it's Mrs. York but her voice sounds like it is echoing. I turn my chair, knocking a bunch of books off of the cart next to me. She sees me and knows something is wrong.

"I need down," I tell her. "I n-need sit d-down." I can hear my voice in my head but it's like someone is talking over an intercom like in the morning announcements. I'm already sitting down, I'm in a freaking wheelchair, but my head doesn't want to let me believe it. I haven't had one of these episodes in a long time, ever since that time I thought I got lost in the mall when I was eight.

"Down, sit. I n-need. Lily." My words jumble and my throat feels dry. I wish I could shut up and calm down. My heart is beating fast in my ears and whole body feels cold, ice cold.

"Mateo, you're having a panic attack. I'm going to wheel you to the nurse's office okay?" Now Mrs. York is blurry.

"Why?" I ask her. But I never get to hear her response.

I wake up in a room and the first thing I notice is that it smells like rubbing alcohol and dirty shoes. I can hear a radio playing music and soft voices talking. Then I hear a familiar sound, a crackling, a walkie-talkie. My eyes swivel toward the sound of the crackling and between some fabric, I see the school nurse talking to two police officers. I'm in the nurse's office. My chest tightens, did I do something? I don't remember getting here from the library. What is going on? I think of getting up and running but then I remember my leg is in a cast. Right now I'm on a bed, slightly obscured by a pink curtain. No one can see that I'm awake, yet.

Sitting in a chair next to the front door is Mrs. York. She looks fine except for maybe looking a little shaken up. She's drinking coffee and listening to the nurse talking to the officers.

I sit up and pull the curtain aside just enough to

be nosy.

Right next to me, sitting on the edge of one of the beds is Marcus Brooks. He's got an ice pack on his hand and there's a reddish lump on his cheek. He looks like he's gotten into a fight, and then it hits me, the police aren't here for me.

He's staring down at his hand and he looks like he wants to punch something... again. I know that feeling, I probably know it better than he does.

The police officers leave and the nurse turns back to Mrs. York and they begin to chat about something. The music coming from a little black radio on the nurse's desk may be on softly but it still muffles what Mrs. York and the nurse are saying to each other.

"*Hey,*" a voice whispers to me. I know it's Marcus but I'm too nervous to even look at him. What does he want with me? We don't know each other.

But I can't be rude. I take a deep breath in, focus on staying calm, and then turn to him. He smiles and it's like all the nervous butterflies and panicky spiders that hide inside of me are gone for now.

"Hi," I say back to him.

"Sorry about your sister," he says. He's saying what everyone says, but it feels different coming out of his mouth. It feels real.

"Thanks," is all I can really say. I'm not good talking to other boys, especially ones I happen to like.

"What happened?" I ask but quickly want to take the question back. It's none of my business, I should know this by now. It's called privacy, Mateo, *privacy*.

But he doesn't seem bothered by the question, so he clears his throat and looks right at me.

"I cracked Jesse Martinez in the face at lunch."

I want to laugh but it seems wrong at the moment. Knowing Jesse for as long as I have, he probably deserved it. That boy has been a pain in a lot of people's butts for a long time. I guess he was bound to get punched sooner or later.

"You think it's funny." He tells me. It's not a question. But he doesn't look mad about it. He cracks another smile.

"I've known him since the third grade. He's an idiot and I'm just surprised it has taken this long for someone to teach him a lesson."

"I don't know if I taught him a lesson. But maybe he'll stop calling people names just because his mom is a cop."

I don't say anything back to him. I just smile. It's a weird one, the kind that can make other boys uncomfortable; at least that's what my dad told me. After I told everybody I liked boys in the sixth grade he told me that not all boys are like me and to be very careful. *Not all boys will look at you the way you look at them*, my dad said, *but if anyone ever tries to hurt you for it, you run those Morales fists through their faces and show them what's up*. Usually my dad wouldn't tell me to get violent because of my IED, but I guess for something like that he'd given me a pass.

But this time it's different. It feels different, because Marcus is smiling back at me.

"Mateo, are you feeling okay? Your mother is waiting in the parking lot for you." Mrs. York walks up to my bed. I look up at her and can tell almost instantly that she knows why Marcus and I are smiling at each other. She winks and then without saying another word helps me up from the bed and back into my chair.

"I'm okay," I tell Mrs. York and let her wheel me toward the front of the office. I turn back and catch Marcus staring at me.

"Bye," he says.

"Bye," I tell him.

Mrs. York leans down and whispers into my ear.

"Don't worry, you'll see him again very soon."

Feeling embarrassed, I shut my mouth the rest of the way back to the library. But what does Mrs. York mean by I'll be seeing him again *very soon*? Just as we're about to cross the quad to the library, a bell rings and the quad begins to fill. Just by people walking toward the front I can tell it's the end of the day.

It occurs to me that I've survived this first day back, even if I had a panic attack and woke up in the nurse's office. At least I didn't break anything or anyone. But then I remember the reason I had the panic attack and realize that I don't want to leave school after all. As a matter of fact, I wonder what Mrs. York would think about me moving into the library for the next four years. I think maybe she'd let me.

There's nothing more uncomfortable and horrifying then being stuck at the dinner table with your parents and annoying sister staring you down. I haven't even eaten anything yet but I feel like I want to throw up already. The clink of forks on the plates makes me flinch and every time Coco twirls himself around my good leg, I get startled and feel like I'm going to pee on myself from being so scared.

So far, no one has said a single thing, but it's like Nina can tell I'm terrified and she thinks it's funny. She keeps snickering and grinning like she can't wait for me to get yelled at. I wonder if she has a bucket of popcorn hiding behind her chair, ready for the show. But I don't understand why she's like this. She's my sister, the only sister I have left, and all she wants to do is hurt my feelings.

"So has any of the news outlets called today?"

Nina is the first to break the silence. But this time, it looks like it is backfiring on her because I can see my mom's face morphing into an angry one, like when someone cuts her off on the freeway.

My mom puts her fork down, cleans the corners of her mouth with a paper towel and then stares head on at Nina, glaring like a vicious cat, ready to attack.

"We're in the middle of eating dinner, Nina. So cállate la boca!" My mom's fist comes down on the table and Nina shakes in her chair, as if a firework has gone off right behind her.

Nina shrivels into herself and then starts poking at her food. This is the first time ever that I've seen her get in trouble and even though it's wrong, I don't feel bad for her.

"Sorry," she says.

I don't know why I let it happen, but I snort a laugh and it's not until I look up from my plate that I realize that I've screwed up. Both my mom and dad are glaring at me like I've just ran over Coco.

"Mateo, you're on very thin ice, me entiendes?" my mom snaps at me, her voice deep and full of frustration. "*Do you understand me?*"

"Yes," I tell her and look back down at my plate.

"Do you really, Mateo?" It's my dad's voice now and I can tell he's extra angry because Coco hurries out from under the table and runs off into the hallway. Lily's cat has always been able to tell when things are about to get serious. I wish I could run off like he does, especially right now.

"I'm sorry, okay?" I look up from my plate and at my mom and dad. I look up because I know he'll yell at me if I don't. I don't like how they're looking at me, like I'm a huge disappointment , like I'm the one who shot Lily.

"We specifically told you not to talk to-"

"I know! But she kept saying things, *bad* things about Lily. She asked me if Lily was in Uncle Paco's gang. Does Uncle Paco have a gang?"

I look at my mom and then my dad, trying to see if they will tell me the truth. But my dad is staring down at his fork. He's not even looking at me anymore. Everybody is silent.

Nina drops her fork onto her plate and turns to me.

"It doesn't matter because it's your fault, Mateo. Whatever they're saying right now about Lily is your stupid fault." Nina is crying now and my throat is going dry.

"NINA!" my dad growls and even I rattle in my wheelchair. "Go to your room."

"But-" Nina tries to save herself, but that's not going to happen tonight.

"GO. TO. YOUR. ROOM." Dad snaps. Nina pushes her chair back and slams it into the table before running off down the hallway. A few seconds later, her bedroom doors slams and she turns on some music.

I don't know why Nina hates me so much right now. I'd like to know, so I could fix it. But I'm not sure that's even possible.

"Mijo, it's not your fault, okay?" My mom reaches her hand across the table and grabs mine. "It's not your fault." She has tears in her eyes and it's making me feel really bad.

"Mateo, you have to understand that what this family is going through right now is really tough. This is really hard on all of us and the last thing we need is for things to get worse."

"I understand." And I do.

"And we're working on fixing this thing with you being locked in the library like some caged animal. It's not right."

"It doesn't really bother me." I say. My dad looks at me. "It's better than having people stare at me and tell me they're sorry all the time. And I like Mrs. York. She's cool." Everything I'm saying is true. I've only been inside the library for one day, but I like it a whole lot better than being the center of attention and pity. But I still know that it's wrong. What the school is doing with me is not okay, but we can all fix this some other time.

My mom and dad need to be focused on what's going on right now with Lily, not with me and that stupid school.

My mom grips my hand and stares at me.

"So, you want to stay in the library?"

"Yes, I'll be okay." I smile at her. I will be okay.

"Are you sure, Mateo?" my dad leans forward under the dining room light that hangs from the ceiling, it makes him look older than he is, and much sadder. "Because we can fix this."

"I'm sure." And that's it. The rest of dinner is quiet and I eat all of my food without feeling like I want to throw it up.

A while later after everyone is asleep, I am

sitting in front of Lily's bedroom door. I can see the light coming out from under the door. No one has shut it off since that night. I reach my hand out to open it... but I can't.

I was the last person in my family to see Lily
alive. The only one who knows about my secret is
Queenie. But this secret is starting to grow inside of me
and it bothers me, like when you have something stuck
in your throat or in your eye. But I'm scared of how my
mom and dad will react. I'm afraid they will be mad at
me, which isn't new, because they're mad at me a lot.
But this is different.

I'm afraid they will blame me.

The night Lily died, I was in her room counting
all of the leaves she had tacked to one of her bedroom
walls. I had counted 104. I remember when my mom
got mad at Lily for covering one her walls in leaves, but
she grew to love it, just like everyone else. The wall was
beautiful, just like Lily.

I was sitting on her bed watching her get ready,

her favorite song "Heroes" by David Bowie was playing on her record player and she was singing along, and I was too. Abuelo Mango gave her that David Bowie record for her birthday when she was my age. She played it over and over ever since.

That night Lily was going with her friends to do some paranormal experiment at the cemetery. The same one she was buried in. Lily had a thing for paranormal stuff too. She used to think abuela Lulu haunted our house, because every so often you could smell roses in a certain part of the house and those were abuela Lulu's favorite flowers. I don't know if I believe in stuff like that. I guess I'd like to think Lily watches us eat dinner, but then that makes me sad.

I remember that night perfectly because she had asked my mom and dad if she could go out with her friends. Even though she was nineteen, she still needed to ask permission. They said no and of course that's where I came in. I was going to help Lily sneak out, like I'd done a few times before. The truth is I never actually did any helping. I was just there for her to talk to and for me that was enough.

"Dumbo, don't worry, I'll be back before Dad gets up for work. It's just me, Amanda, and Julian. I'll be fine."

"You promise?" I had asked.

"Triple scoop at Benny's promise," Lily grinned. A smile I didn't realize I'd never see again.

"With extra Dulce de leche on top?"

"With extra Dulce de leche on top, Dumbo!" her smile was so addictive. Even if you were having a terrible day, Lily could make anyone crack a smile.

"Why are you so scared, Dumbo?"

"I don't know. I wish I could do the stuff you do. I wish I was brave like you."

"Bravery isn't a hard thing to find in yourself, Dumbo. Bravery lives inside all of us. You are already brave, and whether you believe it or not, one day you're gonna need that bravery for something and it will be right here," Lily reached over and poked me in the chest where my heart was.

"How does it feel?" I asked her.

Lily put her hair straightener down and sat down next to me.

"It feels..." Lily stopped to think. "It feels like the sun is shining from inside of you. You get all warm and tingly and you feel like you can do anything. Anything you want. You're not scared, you're not nervous. It's amazing, Dumbo."

"I'm afraid I'll never need it because I'm such a p-word. Jesse called me that yesterday at the park."

"Well, Jesse Martinez is a bully and they're just as scared as everybody else. They're just good at hiding it with being mean to other people."

I laid my head on Lily's shoulder. I wish I could freeze that moment forever.

"But don't worry, Dumbo. One day you'll be brave like me and you'll come running to me screaming

"I'm finally brave like you, Lily!" and I'll flick your ears and we'll go get Benny's ice cream and take on the six gallon ice cream blitz and trust me, Dumbo, you're going to need all the bravery inside you for that." Lily laughed and flicked my ears.

I smiled as I watched her go back to straightening her hair while singing along to Heroes, swaying her head from side to side as if she were in a music video. I didn't know then that it would be the last time I'd see my sister alive.

I didn't want her to go. I wish now that I could've stopped her. I wish I could've been brave enough to say "Lily, please don't go, stay with me. Stay with your little brother because you're going to die tonight and I'm never going to see you again." My bravery failed me then and I have a feeling that it always will. I couldn't be Lily's hero that night. But no matter what, she'll always be mine.

The entire library smells like fresh coffee this Friday morning. Mrs. York is watching something on her laptop and I'm eating my breakfast. I didn't sleep well this week. I kept waking up sweating and wondering if Lily was in her room. I laid there and tried to cry, I tried to push tears out from my eyes. When I woke up in the morning and looked in the mirror, I looked like my dad, except my red eyes weren't from tears, they were from lack of sleep.

The oatmeal is warm this time because I didn't count the oats. Even though my mom made me an egg burrito before my dad dropped me off, I was still hungry when I wheeled myself into school.

I shovel a few globs of oatmeal into my mouth as the library door hisses open. In the reflection of a computer monitor beside me, I can see who it is. It's Marcus Brooks.

I swallow the oatmeal, almost choking as he makes his way toward me. Saving me from embarrassment, Mrs. York hurries out from her office, probably thinking it's another person from the media. She's relieved when she sees that it is Marcus and not the wolf.

"Mr. Brooks, take a seat wherever you like and I will be right with you." Mrs. York goes back into her office, leaving Marcus standing right in front of me.

"Hi, again," I say to him.

"Hey," he smiles. "What are you doing in here?" he probably thinks I've done something bad just like everybody else. I don't blame him. My reputation followed me from middle school to my freshman year and I have a strong feeling it will until I leave this school. I'm the kid with the quick temper. In middle school they used to call me Breaker and I hated it more than anything.

But how am I supposed to explain all of this to him? I could lie, but for some reason, something inside of me is telling me to tell the truth.

"I'm pretty sure you know about me," I tell him. "The school thinks I'm better off inside the library instead of in classes for now. They think I'm going to hurt someone or break a window or something." He doesn't seem scared of me, or worried to be near me. He just looks confused, like he doesn't understand.

"This school is all sorts of messed up. They think just because you're bipolar that you're a threat?" he drags a chair over and sits down across from me, crossing his arms. He seems like he's genuinely trying to be nice, but the sucky thing is that he's wrong already. Everyone thinks I'm bipolar, but I'm not.

"Well, I'm not bipolar. I have IED, which is really different from Bipolar Disorder." I explain it to him how I've explained it to other students when they get it wrong, which is a lot.

"Oh," he combs his hand over his head and I can tell he's embarrassed. "I'm sorry, it's just what everyone says, you know?"

"I get it, it's cool." I smile at him to let him know he's okay and he uncrosses his arms as if to let me know he's okay.

"I know I told you I was sorry about your sister yesterday in the nurse's office, and I am, sorry, but I know you hear it all the time. It starts to get irritating." He's right. It's all people can really say.

I look up from my breakfast tray at him. He's looking down at his hands.

"I'm not going to lie, it does get irritating because I can only say thank you so many times in one day." I tell him the truth.

"Right? You feel like shaking people and asking what they're sorry about. But I guess it's all everyone is taught to say, so you can't really blame them."

Blame... that freaking word. I hate it.

"Yup, or *It was God's plan* or *Things happen for a reason,* I'm so tired of hearing all of that." Marcus finally looks up and at me, his eyes look sad, like he wants to cry but is trying hard not to.

"Or *God needed another angel* doesn't he have enough?" Marcus laughs.

Trying not to make him feel awkward and uncomfortable I laugh with him and then he smiles at me, his eyes even glossier. Something is bothering him, but I don't know if I should say anything. Is what he's feeling even any of my business? He's hurting and I know what that feels like. I just don't know what to do.

So I take in a deep breath, fold my hands on top of the desk to keep myself from fidgeting and open my mouth.

"Are... are you okay?" Out of all the things I could find to say, I say the most annoying thing in the universe. I want to scream at the top of my lungs for asking if he's okay. I hate when people ask me that, even if I'm in a good mood, it's something that tends to ruin my good moods.

He clears his throat two times before he looks directly at me. He's not smiling this time, he looks serious and for a moment I feel like he's going to yell at me and I wish I could sink into my chair, through the bottom, and into the carpet of the library. As I've said, I always ruin everything.

"My dad was killed by a police officer when I was eight." The words come out of his mouth and shoot straight into me like a bullet. My heart feels like it drops into my stomach and all of a sudden I want to throw up the oatmeal. For some reason this brings me right back to the night Lily was killed.

I walked out into the living room after I heard someone screaming.

It was 4:17 in the morning.

Nina ran right past me, dropping her phone on the hallway floor.

I was still rubbing the sleep out of my eyes when I walked out into the living room.

I didn't think anything was wrong until I saw Mom on the floor with Dad holding her in his arms.

"What's wrong?" Nina kept asking over and over until it kept repeating itself like a song's chorus inside of my head.

It wasn't until I walked further into the living room that I saw two police officers standing in the doorway with their heads down.

Right there and then I already knew it was Lily.

I stood there for a while, I don't even remember how long. But I stood there as my dad pulled Nina down to the ground and told her what happened. Soon Nina's cries were blended with my mom's and I was still there, standing, frozen, not crying, not hearing my dad call out to me...

I look up from the table at Marcus and notice that he's waiting for me to speak, to say something.

"I..." but nothing wants to come out.

"Sorry?" Marcus asks.

I swallow hard and nod.

"I know." He smiles at me, but it's not a normal smile this time. It's not one full of happiness. It's one full of pain and sadness. I know it perfectly.

I didn't think in the past nine days that I would meet someone who has gone through what I'm going through right now.

"How did..." I'm trying to ask him how it happened. But I don't know if that is too much. *Is it too far?* I don't want to hurt him.

But when I look at him, he seems to know what I'm trying to ask. He prepares himself to answer by clearing his throat again and looking at me.

"This was before we moved back here. I was with my dad at a corner store. While I was in the bathroom, someone robbed the store and shot the clerk. The police came and thought the dude who robbed the store was my dad..." he stops for a moment, licking his lips and clearing his throat again. This is too hard for him and I want to tell him to stop talking. But he keeps going. "My dad tried to tell them the truth. I could hear everything. I was scared, so I came out of the bathroom and ran toward my dad. He reached out to tell me to stop... and they shot him. Nobody got in trouble for it. It was a mistake, they said. But my dad still ain't here no more."

"Why did they have to die?" I say aloud. I close my eyes and shake my head. I didn't mean for that to come out of my mouth, but it did.

Marcus crosses his arms.

"I don't know. But I wish I knew. I miss my dad."

"I miss my sister." I tell him, my voice small and wobbly.

"Tell me something about her," Marcus says. I look at him in surprise. Ever since Lily died no one wants to talk about her *before* she died. Every time I bring her up *before*, I get shut down. Marcus is the first person, besides Queenie, to bring Lily up like this.

I try to think of something to say, but it's almost

as if Lily can hear me because when I look away from Marcus, the first thing I see is a tree made out of construction paper on a wall near the computer lab.

The leaves are made out of book pages and they are fluttering in the wind from an open window.

"Leaves," I say. "Lily loved leaves."

Marcus is different. Even though I'm only thirteen I've never met anyone like him. I like it but it scares me at the same time, because when I'm around him I feel warm and good and I know it's probably just me that feels that way, so I don't want to get too close to him. I've seen a lot of movies and this is how people end up getting their feelings hurt or heartbroken. But the thing is, my heart is already broken because of Lily. So I really don't think there's nothing left for Marcus to break.

We have a lot of things in common, aside from the gigantic fact that we've both lost someone to police brutality. We both like scary movies, we both like eating cold pizza, and we both hate Jesse Martinez. All I need is for Queenie to meet him, if she hasn't already. I'll know that everything will be okay if she meets him. She'll either give him her Queenie stamp of approval or she won't. Gosh, I hope she does.

I feel bad and weird thinking that Marcus is lucky in a way. He doesn't remember everything from when his dad died, he says a lot of it is still blurry to him. But I'm not that lucky. I remember everything and will for the rest of my life. I'm old enough to keep memories like this and I know that they will hurt me for a really long time.

But whether Marcus knows it or not, he's doing something for me right now. I don't think he's making feel better, I don't think I'll feel better for a really, really long time. But he's making me feel something. I just don't know what it is yet. I can't wait for Monday to come so I can see him again.

My thoughts are interrupted by loud music coming from outside. I roll myself over to my bedroom window and see Uncle Paco's car pull up to the curb out front. He jumps out of the car and spots me staring at him. Uncle Paco is my favorite uncle. My dad has two brothers, Paco whose real name is Pete, and Manuel, who is seven years older than my dad.

Uncle Manny isn't very nice, when he does visit

he's always telling my dad we need a bigger house and that I need to learn how to drive already so I can be a man. I will do that when he stops dressing like a stupid cowboy.

"Hey, Bugs Bunny come out here real quick and help me out," Paco calls out to me. His passenger side door opens and out pops Aunt Terry with a big pot of what I can only hope is Menudo because I freaking hate Pozole. This is interesting to me because Terry rarely comes over and I can't help but feel a little worried about her being here. I just hope it doesn't have anything to do with abuelo Mango.

"On my way," I call out to them and wheel myself out of my room and down the hallway. Before I can get to the front door, Nina jumps out from the kitchen and nearly scares me half to death.

"Don't ruin dinner tonight, Mateo. Uncle Pete and Teresa are our guests."

"Nina, if you don't get out of my way, I will run your feet over again and maybe this time I'll get lucky and break something." I chance it and tell her what I'm really thinking. I'm getting tired of her treating me like crap. This needs to stop.

Nina's mouth drops open in response and she puts her hands on her hips, trying to act like an adult. She's got a long way to go before she gets there.

"You better be glad Mom and Dad aren't in the house to hear you say that to me," she snaps at me, but I can tell she's surprised I even responded to her like that. I want this weird thing between us to stop before it gets worse and one of us says something we will regret for the rest of our lives.

"And you better be glad Uncle PACO isn't in the house to hear you use his real name, because you know he'd make tacos out of your little boyfriend."

"You're disgusting," she sticks her tongue out at me and finally moves out of my way. One other thing that bugs me about Nina is that she can't take a freaking joke and I hate people who can't take jokes.

I head outside, the screen door smacking into the side of my chair. I take the makeshift ramp Paco made down to the front of the house and stop next to Aunt Terry.

"Hola, mijito. Here, take this inside." Terry places the pot on my lap. It's still a little warm.

"Is it Menudo?" I ask, silently praying I'm right.

"Pozole, Mateo. Menudo is for after church on Sundays."

"What she means is after everybody gets tore up on Saturday night and has a hangover." Paco laughs and ruffles my hair.

Terry swats Paco on the arm and shakes her head at him.

"You need to go to church," she wags her finger at him.

"You do," my dad says as he takes a couple of shopping bags full of chips out from Paco's trunk. "And you need to clean this trunk."

Paco laughs and slugs my dad playfully in the chest.

"Paco, now is not the time for joking." My dad snaps.

"Calm down jefe!" Paco pats my dad on the shoulder and I can see my dad's face turning red. Because I know how this will end, I purposefully drop the lid of the pot on the floor and the sound catches everyone's attention.

"Where's Mom?" I ask my dad to help the situation more.

"She forgot cilantro, so she went back to the store."

"Your mama, always forgetful," Terry giggles and heads up the porch. Nina comes out and greets her and they talk about something I can't hear, probably Nina's stupid boyfriend.

My dad walks passed me and heads inside as fast as his feet can take him. I wonder how much convincing it took my mom to get him to let Paco come over since they can't be in a room with each other for ten minutes before they start arguing. Sort of like Nina and I.

I turn back to Paco and smile up at him. He picks up the pot's lid from the floor, shakes it, and then puts it back on top of the pot for me.

"How you doing, Bugs Bunny?" Lily and Paco both had nicknames for me because of my ears, and even though I don't mind, Paco's is a little more embarrassing than Lily's. Just thinking about her, my head falls and I feel sad.

He squats down to my level and knocks my chin up with his hand.

"It's okay to hurt. Pain makes people stronger."

"Does it, really? You're not bullcrapping me?" I look into his eyes. He may look tough with all this tattoos and his baggy Dickies, but deep down Paco is like a teddy bear and he actually listens.

"I promise, I'm not *bullcrapping* you." Paco takes

the pot of Pozole from me and carries it the rest of the way to the house, stopping on purpose every few steps to mess with me. I love my dad, I swear I do. But Paco is like a second dad to me and when he turns back to me, a giant smile on his face, I think of losing him like Lily and then my chest hurts. I don't think I could lose anyone else. I just can't.

Setting the back patio table with paper plates is harder than I thought. The wind keeps yanking them off the table and there's at least fifty napkins fluttering around the backyard like birds. Maybe we should've eaten inside. But then I remember how our dining room table is set and where Lily used to sit. No one would want to sit in her chair.

I look over the table and realize that I need more plates, so I wheel myself back into the house. Searching for the plates, I hear my aunt Terry talking to my dad.

"We're going to move him next week. He can't even remember what day it is sometimes, Victor. You can bring the kids to see him when he moves into Briar Cove." I was right. The only reason she's here is because of abuelo Mango. And it's because they are going to move him into an old home, the one place he used to say he never wanted to end up in.

My dad sees me and knows almost instantly that I heard everything. He tells Terry to hold on and starts walking toward me, but I hurry back out to the patio and realize there's nowhere to run, the rest of the yard is rocks and I can't wheel myself over those.

"Mateo," my dad says behind me. "Listen, abuelo Mango is getting worse and Aunt Terry can't take care of him and her children at the same time. He's going to be better off at Briar Cove."

"He told you guys over and over that he never wanted to go to those stupid places. He said they leave you in your own pee and treat you like crap." My chest hurts and so does my head. I'm trying my best not to get mad, but bad things just keep happening and I don't know how much more I can take before I explode.

"I know, but this is the only option." My dad says. I still have my back turned to him. I can't bring myself to look at his face right now. "We'll go see him on Wednesday next week when he's settled at Briar Cove."

"Whatever," I say and instantly regret it.

"Watch that mouth, Mateo." My dad's voice is stern.

"I'm sorry," I tell him, but I'm not.

The doorbell rings and I wait for my dad to walk away before I turn my chair around. I feel bad for not looking at him while he was talking but I can't help how I feel. Nothing is fair right now and I hate it.

"Mateo," my mom sticks her head out of the sliding door. "Queenie is out front. If you go to her house, be back in an hour to eat."

"Thanks, Mom." I smile at her and instead of going through the house to get to the front, I take the side of the house and prepare myself for guests. I'm not really in the mood to see anyone but if I have to be around anybody right now, I'd rather it be Queenie than anybody else.

But as I turn the corner to the front yard, I see that it's not only Queenie out front, Marcus is right next to her.

"Hey!" Queenie says and Marcus smiles at me.

"What are you guys doing here?" I ask and realize I probably sound more irritated than excited.

"To see you," Queen says, catching my attitude and pointing to Marcus with her eyes. "Marcus didn't know where you lived so I wanted to show him. We live right next door to each other."

It takes me a minute to realize that Marcus is holding something in his hands. He catches me staring and then walks over to me.

"My mom made brownies and wanted me to bring some over to you. They have peanut butter in them."

"Thank you, and tell your mom I said thank you too." I take the container of brownies from him. I'm so nervous I nearly drop them, so I set them down on a porch step so I don't make a fool out of myself.

"I was just showing Marcus where you lived, I

have to get back home because me and my dad are going bowling tonight with Megan. I'll see you guys at school." Queenie is trying to make a getaway but I wheel myself over to her before she heads out of the front gate, leaving Marcus standing by the front door.

"Queenie!" I whisper and she stops and turns back to me with a smile on her face.

"I like him for you. And I think he likes you too." she pokes me in the shoulder.

"How? He was with Dakota."

"Some people can like boys *and* girls, Mateo," she says.

"True," I tell her and turn to look at him. He's staring down at his shoes and messing with his shirt. I wonder if he can hear what Queenie is saying.

"So be happy for a little while. I know you don't feel like it's right to be, but Lily wouldn't want you feeling bad, she'd want you to be happy." Queenie always knows the right things to say and sometimes, I get mad I didn't think of them first.

"Thanks, Queenie." I smile at my best friend. I really don't know what I'd do without her.

"There's that smile," Queenie winks and then sprints down the street and turns the corner. I hear the crunching of the rocks behind me and prepare myself to look up at Marcus.

"Did you happen to hear any of that?" I ask.

"All of it," he says and I want to crumble to pieces and float away with the last of the September wind.

Marcus is walking beside me on the sidewalk and we've been on silent since leaving my front yard. The fact that he heard everything Queenie was saying makes me feel so awkward and embarrassed. I don't know what to say to make it less weird without it being forced and that would be so much worse.

"The car parked on the curb in front of your house is nice," he says and I'm so glad Marcus decided to speak first.

"That's my uncle Paco's car, he calls it Betty and it's candy-apple-red chrome."

"It's really cool." Great now we're talking about Paco's car. If I don't do something we'll be talking about it for the rest of our time hanging out. I decide to take my turn, but instead of picking a better topic, I nervously say the stupidest thing I can think of.

"Why did you and Dakota break up?" I want to wheel myself into the middle of the street for saying that. "I'm sorry, that's none of my business."

"Nah, it's okay. I just didn't feel the same anymore and she was too much for me to handle. My mom told me, that white girl is going to get you into trouble, and she was right. She brought a bottle of vodka to school and thought it was cool to drink between classes. Plus she can be really mean and I don't like being pinched and pushed around or called names. I'm fine, but she still thinks we'll get back together and I can't wait until she gets it through her head that it's over-over."

From afar they looked like the perfect couple, but I guess looks can be super deceiving and from the sound of it, he got away before she took him down with her.

"I know the vigil is soon. How are you doing?" Marcus does me a favor and changes the subject.

"I don't really know. I'm just going day by day. I

still don't feel good and I'm still mad that nothing is being done about what happened to Lily. I heard my mom and dad talking to Mr. Curtis, our lawyer last night and he said the investigation isn't going well." When I heard that last night it hurt me even more.

"Sadly, that's how the system works. I hate it, but as much as people try, it doesn't seem to do a thing." Marcus kicks a chunk of asphalt off the curb.

"They said the police officer said it was a mistake. So how can we blame him?" I ask. I'm curious to know how he feels about it.

"Do *you* blame him?" Marcus looks down at me.

"I don't know. That's the problem I've been having," I tell him, hoping it doesn't make him mad at me.

"To be honest, I really don't think it's about *blaming* someone. To me it's about taking responsibility. We're allowed to make mistakes in life because that's just life. But there will always be repercussions for our actions no matter what."

"Out of everyone trying to make it make sense to me, you're the first person to actually do it. Is this why you're captain of the debate team?" I ask him.

"Might be," he chuckles. "But in all seriousness, what I'm saying is true. People tend to let anger speak for them instead of trying to speak for themselves."

"So, he should be held accountable for what he did?" I ask. I feel like the officer does, my sister is gone and she's never coming back. He's still here and he shouldn't just get away with it.

"Absolutely," Marcus says and I realize we've been standing on the corner talking. I was so engrossed in what he was saying that I didn't notice we weren't moving anymore. I love Queenie, but she's never made it make this much sense to me, but then again we haven't been hanging out as much since Lily died.

"Hey look! It's Marcus and Mateo, don't they look so cute together?" I turn and see Jesse Martinez and his group of dummies heading our way on their bikes.

They skid to a stop in the street and out of the corner of my eye, I see Marcus make a fist. There's definitely still some tension between them. Jessie has his dark brown hair slicked back and his red shirt has what looks like mustard stains on it.

"Go away, Jesse." I tell him and without warning he kicks the wheel on my chair.

"Shut up, cripple boy."

"Leave him alone," Marcus steps in front of me. Jesse gets off his bike and puffs his chest out. I know they're going to fight. But I don't know what to do about it? I'm in a chair and I don't have my phone.

"What are you going to do about it?" Jesse pushes up against Marcus with his chest and Jesse's friends start rooting for Jesse to kick Marcus's butt.

"I thought I taught you a lesson at lunch, Martinez." Marcus pushes Jesse back into the street, Jesse's bike topples to the ground.

"You guys, stop!" I say.

"Hey pachucos! What's the problem here?" My
uncle Paco comes up from behind me and nearly scares
me to death. He must've seen what was going on from
down the street.

"Hey Paco," Jesse says, acting like they're best
friends.

"Jesse, go home and take your friends with you. I
don't wanna have to tell your mom you're out here
starting fights, especially with people who can't defend
themselves." Paco puts a hand on my chair. I'm grateful
for Paco showing up, but he's embarrassing me now.

Instead of responding, Jesse picks up his bike
and takes off down the street with his friends, but not
before turning back, pointing to Marcus and making a
slit throat gesture. I swallow hard and follow Paco and
Marcus back to my house.

"I'm Paco, Mateo's uncle, the cool one." Paco
shakes hands with Marcus.

"Marcus Brooks," Marcus says, a little intimidated by Paco.

"Pam's son?" Paco asks.

"Yeah," a smile forms on Marcus's face.

"I went to high school with her back in the day before she moved to Cali. You hungry? Come eat with us in the back. Mateo's parents won't mind."

Marcus turns to me for confirmation.

I smile and nod, giving him my okay. Maybe Marcus being here will put a stop to any fighting that would be sure to happen tonight.

Sitting in the library on Monday, I'm thinking about Marcus. But not because I'm sure I like him, I'm thinking about him because of what he said on Saturday. The news has been saying they will update everyone when the time comes, and so does our lawyer. My dad is getting angrier day by day and my mom seems to be getting sadder. I wish I could fix this somehow.

My phone vibrates and I see it's a text from Queenie.

Marcus was jumped last night. He's okay but his arm is broken and he won't be coming to school this week. His mom told me.

I don't have to wonder, I already know who did it. Jesse Martinez. Anger takes charge and I can feel my face grow hot. I text back, *It was Jesse.*

Queenie texts back and says she knows and she'll see me at lunch.

I sit in silence, thinking of how amazing Marcus is and how ugly Jesse must be to intentionally hurt someone so kind. It's got me thinking about the officer who killed Lily. *Why do people do these things?*

I text Queenie, *Is Jesse here today?*

Five minutes later she texts back, *yes.*

I wonder if Jesse got away with it because his mom is a cop? If he did then that's not fair and he should be held accountable for what he did. Marcus is hurt and that makes me angrier than I've been since Lily passed away. Mrs. York went to go make copies in front office so I'm alone. Quickly I grab my jacket, roll it up and shove some of it into my mouth. I bite down hard and scream. I scream even harder and then find that I can't stop. The front doors to the library hiss open and giving it all my strength I stop screaming. But it's not Mrs. York, it's Queenie.

She can tell I've just had a mini-episode and hurries up to me to hug me.

"I'm so sorry, Mateo. I know this is a lot."

Instead of saying anything, I just let Queenie hold me for a while. It reminds me of Lily and right now I feel like I need this. The sound of the library doors opening startles us and Queenie lets go.

"What's going on? Is everything okay?" Mrs. York asks, balancing a giant stack of paper in her arms.

"Here, let me help you with that." Queenie takes a chunk of the stack from Mrs. York and follows her into her office.

The lunch bell rings and I turn and see Queenie and Mrs. York talking. I know where Jesse is going to be right now and want to say something to him. But I know Queenie won't let me. I make sure they're still talking before I silently wheel myself toward the library's entrance and then slip out undetected.

Out in the quad people are already gathering,

but I don't see Jesse or his stupid friends yet. I wheel myself further from the library, I'm guessing Queenie or Mrs. York haven't noticed that I'm gone yet. Eventually the B building doors fling open and Jesse comes through with his friends behind him.

Gathering up all the courage in me, plus the anger, I push myself through the crowds of people, running over peoples feet and backpacks as I go. I'm determined to get to Jesse. I turn and see Queenie and Mrs. York surveying the crowds of students for me. Finally, I'm twenty feet in front of Jesse.

"Jesse!" I call out and he turns to me, the smirk falling from his face.

"What do you want cripple boy?"

"I know what you did to Marcus."

"Yeah?" Jesse says and walks up to me. "Do you want me to break your other leg? Cuz I can if I want to." He smirks at me, trying to be all macho in front of his friends. I'll never understand bullies or why they do mean things to people and what it does for them.

111

"What's wrong with you?" I ask him.

"Get away from me, Mateo. You don't have your boyfriend, your uncle, or your *dead* sister to help you right now."

"Jesse, that's enough bro," one of his friends says, knowing Jesse is going too far, which he is. But I can't put my parents through anything else, so I have to go before things get out of hand.

"Idiot," I say and before I do something stupid I turn and start to wheel myself away.

"Your sister shouldn't have been in that graveyard that night. Officer Woods was just doing his job and your sister was being stupid. She deserved what she got."

I stop myself in the middle of the quad and turn back to him. Everyone around me is so silent that I can hear birds chirping. I'm not sure what I'm about to do and I'm more scared than I've ever been.

"What did you say?" I scream at him and he stumbles back, probably realizing what he just said to to me was really bad.

"Mateo, stop!" I hear Queenie but I ignore her. Quicker than I thought possible I leap out of my chair and throw myself at Jesse, taking him down to the ground.

Students crowd around us and Jesse decks me across the cheek. I reel my arm back and my fist meets Jesse's face. Soon I'm punching and punching him while screaming at the top of my lungs. Now people are dispersing, because I probably sound crazy. Jesse cries out for me to stop but I can't.

Before I have time to realize it, I'm being lifted off of Jesse and shoved back into my chair by school security. Queenie is beside me now but when I turn to look at her everything goes black.

I passed out and when I woke in the nurse's office, my mom and dad were standing over me, but they weren't angry, they were worried, which to me is even worse. I promised I'd be okay, I told them I wouldn't have to go back on my meds. I ruined everything and I can't help but feel like Lily would be disappointed in me right now. I knew I wouldn't be able to stop if I hurt Jesse, but I did it anyway and I feel disgusted with myself.

Mom and Dad are in the principal's office with Jesse's mom and interestingly, they've made Jesse and I sit right next to each other outside the office. But I'm calmer now and Jesse is weirdly quiet.

"You hit hard," Jesse says, finally breaking the silence.

I don't look at him. "So do you." I raise a hand and touch the cut on my cheekbone where Jesse hit me.

"Yeah, but you were like a robot, you didn't stop."

I risk it and turn to him. I busted his lip and he has a black eye. He doesn't look so tough now. He looks scared and different.

"I didn't mean what I said about your sister. I

was mad and I knew it would hurt you so I said it anyway. Lily was cool. She was really cool." I'm almost in shock as I listen to him talk. As long as I've know him, he's never been this nice to me.

"Why are you so mean?" I ask him. He shakes his head and looks down, twisting the bottom of his shirt.

"Because I have to be. Everybody thinks cuz my mom's a cop I'm a snitch or something. So I'm mean instead. If they're scared of me, I guess I can't get hurt."

Even though I don't like it, I feel bad for Jesse.

"I don't think it works like that though, but I get it. Everybody's scared of me too, Jesse. But I don't bully people to make it better."

"Well, from what people saw today I wouldn't be surprised if people are more scared of you than me for now on." He laughs and turns to me. "You're not that bad after all, Mateo."

"Thanks, I guess." I crack a laugh. "But what

about Marcus?"

"That actually wasn't my *all* my fault. I was just trying to scare him and he hit me. So I pushed him and he ran at me. I moved out of the way. He tripped over his basketball and practically flew in the air. I ran before he could get up and get me. I didn't know he broke his arm."

"Well, you should go apologize anyway. I'm sure he'd appreciate it."

"I guess I should." he says, now he is looking at me. "And I'm sorry about Lily. As I said, she was really cool. She helped me build my bike a couple of years ago before it got stolen and I had to get a new one."

"Lily was helpful like that," I tell him.

"Yeah, she was." Jesse says.

Our conversation is cut short by the appearance of our parents, my mom and dad are staring at me with worry again. Gosh, I wish they'd stop making me feel bad.

"Mateo, I'm sorry for Jesse's actions today. But he said something he shouldn't have. Officer Woods's name has not be released to the public yet and I'd appreciate it if you didn't tell anyone. This could put him in a lot of danger. He has two little girls and a wife that could get hurt."

"I understand," I tell Jesse's mom. I turn to Jesse and he nods, knowing what I'm about to say. "But he said that out loud in the quad, I'm pretty sure the people around us heard him."

"Oh my god, this can't be happening right now." Jesse's mom puts her hands over her face and shakes her head.

"Maybe no one will remember hearing it, Isabel." my mom says to her.

"I hope not. But thank you for your cooperation, Mateo. I'm sorry about Lily," she says and tells Jesse it's time to go. I'm sure he's in a lot of trouble.

My dad walks up to me and squats down to my

level. I prepare myself to hear about how much of a disappointment I am and how I will be put back on my meds. I guess I deserve it.

"Are you okay?" my dad asks me. There are tears in his eyes.

"I'm okay. Dad, why are you crying?"

"I was scared, Mateo. When they called us and told us you got into a fight and were passed out in the nurses office, I freaked out."

"Me too, mijo." my mom says and squats down next to my dad.

"We can't lose anyone else, okay?" Dad is crying now and so is my mom.

"I'm sorry," I tell him. "I promise I'll never scare you guys like that ever again."

"Okay," my dad says and pulls my mom and I into a hug.

It's been a week and a half since I got suspended from school. My mom and dad grounded me but I still get to go to the candlelight vigil since it's coming up super soon. I know Queenie has been working so hard on it with a local civil rights group and I need to be there. Queenie finally gave Marcus my number and he told me that Jesse went over and they talked. I wish I could see him in person but I'm not allowed to leave the house alone and no one is allowed over.

After the fight, I went to the doctor for my leg check up and I don't need the wheelchair anymore, which I guess is a good thing. But I'm missing it now because these crutches I have to use now hurt my armpits so bad.

Today we're finally going to see abuelo Mango at Briar Cove. Afterward we're supposed to go to Petey's Pizzeria and I'm surprised we're going out to eat. We haven't since the week before Lily died. She was the one who always made sure we ate out at least once a week. It was our family time, but now that she's gone I don't know how it is going to feel without her.

Abuelo Mango is sitting in his wheelchair when we arrive. His room is bright and the walls have this brown and cream wallpaper. It looks like a hospital room. His bed looks like the ones in the hospital too. I'm glad there's at least a record player on the bedside table. Nina is already here. She got here an hour before we did because Gage dropped her off.

"Hi, abuelo Mango," I say from behind him. He turns around and smiles at me. His eyes are huge and happy, I've missed him so much.

"Dumbo!" he says and then he notices my crutches and cast. "What happened?"

"He fell out of that tree at the funeral, you remember papa?" my dad says and pats abuelo Mango on his back.

"Where is my little flower, my Lily?" abuelo

Mango asks, trying to look over my shoulder. My mom stifles a cry and walks out of the room. My dad goes after her. Nina is sitting on the edge of his abuelo Mango's bed, texting someone on her phone.

"She passed away, abuelo Mango. Remember, I told you," Nina tells him.

"Oh yes, I remember now." Tears are hovering at the rims of his eyes. "I miss her a lot. My Lily."

"I do, too," I tell him and give him a hug.

"I'm starving! I want something sweet but they won't let me have anything like that. The vending machines are in the lobby and they catch you if you try to be sneaky," abuelo Mango laughs. Before I can say anything Nina opens her mouth.

"I'll go get you something from the machines, what do you want?"

"A Reese's and a Snickers!" abuelo Mango says and winks at Nina.

"I'll be right back then." Nina hurries out of the room. I have a feeling she doesn't really want to be here. She was never really close to abuelo Mango and that was by her choice. He always tried to include her in our trips or when we'd have a movie night, but she never wanted to hang out.

"Do you like it here?" I ask him and he looks out of the sliding door window.

"I like the view and the sunset. I don't wake up in my pee, so I suppose that is a good thing," abeulo Mango chuckles.

"Yeah, I think so too." I laugh and he pats me on the shoulder.

"Lily would've liked the sunset," abuelo Mango says.

"I know she would've." I say. "It's hard with her not here."

"I know. I lost my brother Roberto when I was nine, you remember I told you? But I never told you how. He was being chased by the police because he was in the wrong place at the wrong time. They chased him until they cornered him and ran him over."

I've never heard this story, not even from my dad. Abuelo Mango knows the pain of loss better than me. He lost his brother, his parents, and his own wife. He's went through a lot of loss. I don't know how he got through it.

"Did it hurt, losing him?" I ask abuelo Mango.

"Oh yes, Mateo. But the pain never really goes away, it just grows dull. But going on with life makes dealing with the pain easier day by day. Soon you'll smile at the memories instead of wanting to cry."

"But I haven't cried for Lily yet," I confess. I haven't told anybody this, not even Queenie. "I try to make myself cry, but it never works."

"You will, and it will happen at a moment so overwhelming that you simply can't control your emotions and bam! Waterworks. It doesn't make you a bad person to have not cried yet, Mateo."

"I needed to hear that," I smile at him. He wrinkles his face into a smile.

"Needed to hear what?" I hear my dad ask as he reenters the room, without my mom.

"Where's Mom?" I ask, trying to take the attention off our conversation.

"She's going to wait in the car with Nina. She doesn't feel too good. But Nina told me to give you these." He hands abuelo Mango the Reese's and Snickers bars. And then out of nowhere he hands me a Twix. "She said to give this to you."

I stare down at the candy bar. My favorite candy bar. Nina would never do something like this.

"Really?" I ask.

"Really," my dad says and I can see in his face that he's being truthful. So why is Nina caring all of a sudden? Maybe she's finally growing up?

"Papa, I brought you a Beatles record." my dad pulls a record out of the bag slung over his shoulder and walks over to the player. Abuelo Mango follows him and they listen to the record together.

My dad looks happy, which I haven't seen a while. He's still feeling the pain of Lily's loss but he's living life, like abuelo Mango said. Lily wouldn't have wanted us to stop living anyway. She would've wanted us to do the things we normally do and she would probably be standing next to my dad and abuelo Mango listening to Let It Be by The Beatles. A part of me thinks she is doing that right now. As a matter of fact, I know she is.

I never win anything, especially against Nina. So while we're on our eighth game of air hockey, when I actually win a few times, I know something is up. Why is she being so nice to me? She's not talking to me but she's not being mean to me. It's weird and I don't know how to react to it.

We've never really had a good brother and sister relationship and I never understood why. I'm only thirteen but I'm not stupid, I notice if my own sister doesn't like me or want me around. It hurts my feelings but there's nothing I can do about it. I can't tell on her, what would that do? Force her to be nice? Lily is gone and all I have is Nina, but it doesn't feel that way.

I'm building the courage up inside as we play because I want to know why she's being nice, why she's acting like I exist for once. But I also don't want to ruin this time we've been spending together. But something inside of me is telling me to say something. Maybe it's Lily, maybe she's somehow letting me know that it's okay to speak to Nina.

"Why are you being so nice to me?" I ask.

Nina stops playing, the air hockey puck gliding on its own toward the side of the machine. It bumps the side and hovers there for a moment. Nina isn't looking at me, but she's about to say something.

"What are you talking about?" she asks me nervously, still not looking at me.

"You're never this nice to me. You practically hate me and I-"

"-I don't hate you," she cuts me off. "I'm not *evil*, Mateo."

"Well, you sure don't like me then."

"You know what? I'm tired now. I'm gonna go eat pizza." she drops the hockey pusher on the table, turns and walks off.

There I go messing things up again. I tried, I just want to know why she's so mean to me and why all of a sudden she wants to treat me like a brother. Did Nina's death do something to her? Maybe one day I'll know. But I want to know *now*.

"Nina, wait." she stops, but doesn't turn back to me. "Just talk to me, please."

I watch my sister fidget with her blouse for a while before she finally turns around and walks over to a red and blue bench near the ticket collecting machine. It's a lot more quiet there. She sits down and gestures for me to come over.

Sitting down next to her I grow nervous. I haven't sat this close to her in a long time. Usually at dinner she's a few feet from me and in the car she sits in the seat behind the regular back seat. So this feels weird to me, but I don't hate it.

"I know I haven't been the best sister," Nina says.

"Gee, you think?" I laugh, trying to break the

nervous tension.

"Mateo, I'm trying to be serious," she snaps at me.

I nod and turn to her. She takes in a deep breath and looks at me. She looks so much like Lily, except Nina's eyes are more honey-colored.

"I had a talk with abuelo Mango while we waited for you guys to come. He made a lot sense about things and... it got me thinking..." Nina starts pulling at fringe hanging from the bottom of her blouse. "I'm sorry for being such a.. mean sister."

I almost feel like I'm staring at a stranger, because this just can't be happening. As long as I can remember Nina's basically hated me. So her talking to me and apologizing to me doesn't seem real. But it is and it's really all I ever wanted.

Nina clears her throat and keeps going. "Before you were born, Lily and I were inseparable. We did everything together and then you came along and Lily started helping Mom take care of you and never wanted to play with me. But it didn't stop there, as we got older she just kept picking you over me. Or at least that's how I felt.

But after she died, I started remembering all the things we did, all the late nights watching movies, shopping together, just talking to each other. I was just jealous, even though I hate to admit it. I'm a sucky sister, but I plan to fix that. You're my little brother and even though you make me super mad most of the time, I love you."

"I love you too, Nina." I smile up at my sister.

"You do?" she asks, tears in her eyes.

"I do." And just as insane as Nina being nice to me, David Bowie's Heroes starts playing in the arcade area. I take it as a sign from Lily and I can see that Nina does too. Nina leans in and hugs me which if I can remember has never happened. She smells like cotton candy and hairspray. I hug her back, hard. She lets go of me and tells me she's going to the table to eat.

I watch her walk back to the table and notice

that my mom and dad have been watching us and they are smiling. I get up, put my crutches under my arms and start walking toward the table.

"But I want this one sissy!" I hear a boy's voice and stop. I turn to see a little boy with what looks like his older sister at the prize counter. He's pointing to a big blue bear that is cradling a plastic bottle of glow-in-the-dark slime.

A pain comes to life in my chest and for a moment I think I'm going to cry, but it's just seeing a boy and his sister that makes me feel sad. It reminds me of Lily and I so much.

The last night I saw her resurfaces and I turn to look at my mom, dad, and Nina sitting at a table with a giant pizza talking about something. I didn't want to tell anyone about the last night I saw her, about how I was the last one to see her alive.

But seeing that little boy and his older sister struck something in me. If I don't tell anyone now, it will just stay a secret and I hate secrets. But what will my family think of me after I tell them. *Will they blame me?*

I slide onto the bench next to Nina and my mom hands me two slices of pizza on a flimsy paper plate. I take one bite and then clear my throat.

"I have something to tell you guys," I'm looking down, but I know at any moment my dad will tell me to look up, so I beat him to it and they are all staring at me.

"What is it, mijo?" my mom asks. I look at her and she seems normal in a way and I have a feeling I'm about to ruin that for her.

"If this is about Marcus, we already know you like him, Mateo." Nina tries to toss in something funny but my dad glares at her and she throws her hands up in surrender.

"I was with Lily the night she died." I say. It feels like a giant weight has been lifted off of my chest. I look up and see my mom's face fall a bit. My dad looks sad and Nina looks surprised for some reason. "I was in her room and I was watching her get ready."

"And you've been keeping this to yourself all this time?" Mom asks. "There's nothing wrong with you hanging out with your sister the night she... there's nothing wrong with it, Mateo." my mom looks like she's going to cry.

"But I was the last one to see her alive, I could've stopped her from going with her friends that night." I feel like I'm causing pain to my family right now and I just want to take it all back.

"You weren't the last one to see her alive." Nina says. I turn to her and she has tears running down her face. "I helped her sneak out the back door that night, while Mom was in the living room talking to Aunt Terry on the phone."

I'm staring at Nina in shock. All this time, I thought I was the last one to see Lily alive. I kept blaming myself in a way, hurting myself with this secret. All along, I wasn't alone and neither was Nina.

"Hey," my dad snaps his fingers at us. "Listen to me. Neither of you couldn't have stopped anything.

Don't blame yourself for what happened, okay?"

Nina and I nod at him.

My dad's phone vibrates on the table and he clears his throat before picking it up. My dad says hello and instantly his face morphs into a distressed look. He's listening intently and my mom even leans over to try and hear who is on the other end.

"What? Where?" my dad's voice cracks. "Okay, I'll be right there. Don't let him leave!" He hangs up with whoever it is, shoves his phone in his pocket, and then jumps up from the table.

"Victor, what's going on?" my mom asks, grabbing her purse.

"My idiot brother," my dad says. "Someone told him the police officer's name and he wants to do something stupid right now. Come on, let's go!"

"It's Paco, you know him, he's all talk," my mom says, putting her purse over her shoulder. It's true, I've never known him to do anything really bad. But this is about Lily and I'm afraid that he's about to do something he will regret for the rest of this life.

"Elena, he has a gun."

The only thing I can think of is that someone from school told Paco the officer's name. If Jesse would've kept the officer's name to himself this wouldn't be happening right now. But thinking about Paco, I'm sure he would've found out his name anyway. Either way, something like this was bound to happen. I just wish it wasn't. We don't need to lose anybody else.

My dad practically flies down Aunt Terry's street, Nina and I holding onto our seat belts for dear life. My mom is trying to calm my dad down, but he's not listening to her. He just keeps driving and cursing under his breath. He looks more scared than angry, because he knows if he doesn't stop Paco, something bad will happen.

When he pull up to Aunt Terry's house, my dad pulls onto the lawn and before he can jump out of the van my mom grabs him by his shirt.

"Don't get too mean with him, he lost his niece, Victor."

Without answering her my dad pulls his shirt out from her hand and bolts up the lawn as the front screen door creaks open. Paco walks out and I see the hilt of a gun poking out from his Dickies. This is bad.

"Get away from me, jefe. I need to do this." Paco is walking toward his car.

"No, you don't Pete!" my dad snaps at him. That's the first time I've heard him call Paco by his real name and my dad has been super angry at him sometimes.

"He's going to get away with it, Victor! You know how this works, we grew up on the police having their way with us and I'm not going to stand for it anymore."

"He has a family!" my dad yells.

"And what about us, Victor? Lily's not here anymore. My freaking first born niece, man! I'm supposed to die before her! You're supposed to die before her! This is not how it's supposed to be." Paco is crying now and I've never seen him do that before. Not even at Lily's funeral. He's always been the tough one and now he looks so hurt that it makes me angry.

"I know, okay? I get it, but killing him is not going to make things right." My dad tries to calm him down but Paco isn't going to back down.

"It will for me," Paco says and opens his car door. My dad runs up and yanks him out of the car's doorway, the gun flying into the air and landing in the bush by the porch.

Now they're fighting on the lawn and Aunt Terry is screaming. Mom jumps out of the car and starts pulling at my dad, telling him to stop. Nina is holding her hands over her ears and looks so scared.

Angry and frustrated, I try to hop out of the car, one of my crutch's is stuck in the seat belt so I just use one and limp up the lawn toward my dad and my uncle fighting like kids on the ground.

"Stop!" I yell. Aunt Terry and her husband Jaime are trying to break them apart too, my mom even tears my dad's shirt trying to pull him away from Paco. "Dad, Paco! Stop it!" but they aren't listening to me.

My dad pushes Paco into the ground and it doesn't seem like they're going to stop anytime soon. Someone has to do something before one of them gets hurt. I hobble over to the bush the gun flew into and reach inside. I don't know what I'm doing, but I need to do something.

My hand closes on the gun and I pull it out. I remember seeing a movie once where a guy shot a gun at the sky to stop people from arguing. Maybe that will work for me.

No one notices that I'm holding the gun in my hand, so I point it to the sky and take a deep breath before pulling the trigger.

POP!

The sound echoes into the night and dogs in the neighborhood start barking. Just like in the movie, my dad and Paco stop fighting and now they're all staring at me.

"Mateo, what are you doing?" my mom yells. "Put the gun down."

"Put it down, son." my dad commands.

"Are you guys going to stop fighting?" I ask them.

My dad and Paco get up from the lawn and walk toward me.

"Let me see it," Paco says.

"No," I pull away. "You're going to go to jail or get killed if you go shoot Officer Woods. I can't lose anybody else, okay Uncle Paco?"

Paco looks into my eyes, his own swollen with tears. He doesn't have to say anything. I know he's not going to use the gun after all.

But instead of giving it to him, I give it to

Terry's husband and he and Terry take it inside the house. I turn and see my dad and Paco hugging and crying onto each others shoulders. My mom comes up to me and slaps me on the back of the head.

"Don't you ever do anything like that ever again, do you understand me?"

"Yes, Mama." I tell her and she hugs me long and hard.

Nina is standing by the car, black makeup running down her cheeks.

I let go of my mom and go up to her.

"I was scared, too." I tell her.

"But you shot the gun into the air, that's brave." she swipes tears from her eyes. As strong and collected as my sister likes to make herself seem. She's still a child deep down, just like me.

"I guess it's brave," I say and turn back to my dad and Paco hugging.

They look so small on the lawn, like little kids again, and I see the love they both have for each other. No matter how many times they argue or how many fights they get into. They love each other more than anything and for the first time I can clearly see that tonight. Lily wouldn't believe it if she saw it. Or maybe she would've. But today has sparked something inside of me. I want to do something big for Lily, something to help people see that the media and police department are wrong. I want to say something, I just don't know how. But I know someone who does.

Two days later after begging and begging my mom and dad are letting Queenie and Marcus come over. I told Queenie about my plan and she's on board. She suggested we post a video on Facebook because videos on there tend to get a lot of attention. I didn't tell Mom or Dad or Nina.

I know it might make them mad, but I need to do this. I need to do this for Lily. I'm just sad that it took me this long to want to be brave for her. But I feel like she's smiling at me right now, maybe even giving me a round of applause for finally having the courage to speak up.

After the incident at Aunt Terry's house, Paco has calmed down a lot. He hasn't tried to do anything else and he even had a conversation with my dad on the phone last night, something I never see happen. Nina hasn't said much to me, but she smiles and winks and even flicks me on my ears which is all I could ask for right now.

The night I shot the gun at the sky, I heard my mom crying in the dining room. It was late at night and I guess she didn't think anyone was up.

I crept into the kitchen as best as I could with my crutches and saw that she was sitting at the kitchen table in Lily's chair. She was holding one of Lily's inhalers.

I felt like I was being intrusive to her so I tried to sneak back off to my room but one of my crutches hit the stove and she turned and saw me.

"Oh, Mateo. Are you okay? Why are up so late?" she asked, clearly embarrassed that I'd caught her crying at the table. I didn't want to lie so I walked over to the table and sat down across from her.

"I heard you crying. I came out to see if you were okay," I told her and she swiped tears from her already swollen eyes.

"I found this in the cabinet all the way in the back." Mom held up the inhaler. "It's from when she first got Asthma."

"I miss her, Mom. I miss her so much."

"I know, mijo. I still find it hard to believe she's not here anymore. But I'm trying my best to keep my head up for you and Nina." she reached across the table and patted my hand.

"You don't need to be Wonder Woman for us. If you feel sad, feel sad."

"Okay," she smiled at me. "You want some left over Arroz Con Leche? You know your aunt Terry makes it better than me." she got up, walked over to the stove and started to pour a butter container of Arroz Con Leche into a pot.

"Yeah," I told her. Even though I wasn't that hungry, I let her warm up some for me. I can't imagine how she must feel having lost her own child, especially her first born.

I wish I could soften the pain for her and my dad. Seeing them so hurt makes me even more driven to do something about all of this.

Hearing a familiar giggle, I'm pulled out of my thoughts. I look out of my bedroom window and see Queenie and Marcus walking up the driveway, a neon green cast on Marcus's right arm. I'm nervous, but I can do this.

The doorbell rings and I hear my mom let them in and tell them I'm in my room. I look around and realize I didn't get to clean my room, so I start kicking things under my bed with my good leg and nearly fall out of the window trying to make my room look decent.

Marcus walks in first, a giant smile on his face. Queenie is behind him, carrying a fake biology project. It was the only way my mom would let them come over. I told her they needed my help with it for class.

"How is your leg?" Marcus asks, sitting down on my bed.

"It's getting better. I think I have a couple more

weeks before they can take it off. It itches like crazy. How's your arm?" I nod at his cast and he puts his other arm over it, clearly embarrassed.

"I still feel like an idiot. But thanks again for talking to Jesse, he seems like a different person now. It's weird. He even says hi to me in school." Marcus laughs and Queenie joins in.

"Yeah, you must've knocked the bully out of him or something." Queenie says as she sets up her phone's tripod. I swear Queenie could run the world if she wanted.

I want to tell them about my conversation with Jesse, but I feel like it's something I need to keep to myself. He confided in me and I don't want to ruin or disrespect that.

"I guess," I chuckle and let them believe what they want. It's better that way.

After Queenie has set up her phone, Marcus pulls my desk chair in front of it. It looks like I'm about to do an interview, but it's just me in front of the camera. I'm nervous, but I'm not letting it stop me. I want to be Lily's hero now.

"Do you know what you want to say?" Queenie asks.

"I do, I'm just a little scared of what Mom, Dad, and Nina are going to say if they find out." I twist my fingers. "But I'm not scared to talk about Lily."

"They're going to be mad, I won't lie. But they'll get over it, especially if it will help Lily. You've got this, Mateo," Queenie reassures me. I look at her and see the fire in her eyes, the fire I've always known Queenie to have. And I know now that she can see it in my eyes too.

"I'm ready," I tell her and Marcus.

Queenie walks over to her phone and hits the record button. I see myself in the camera and take a deep breath, getting ready to release all that I've been holding back and how I feel. This is for my sister and for all of the victims and families of victims everywhere.

One day you'll be brave like me, Lily once said.

For me, today is that day. A cozy warm feeling rushes through me, like when you're standing outside when the sun sets in the fall. A chill runs down my spine. This is it.

"My name is Mateo Morales, and Lily Morales is my sister."

When I was nine, I broke a special vase my mom's abuela had given to her when she was younger. I cried about it for hours. I stopped crying when Lily got home from hanging out with her friends and helped me put the vase back together. To this day, my mom has no idea I broke the vase, so whenever I look at it now I think of Lily.

I feel like my family is that vase now and I have put help put us back together, which is why I had to make that video.

It took me twenty minutes to say what I needed to say and I still feel like it wasn't enough. Queenie said it was enough and that this will do something. Marcus told me that I'm the bravest person he knows now.

It's been three hours since Queenie and Marcus posted the video and left. My mom and dad left an hour ago and aren't home yet and Nina is in her room, talking to Gage on the phone.

I'm standing in front of Lily's bedroom door with my hand on the knob. My heart is in my throat but I know that I need to go inside. Just like when I made the video, I take a deep breath and open the bedroom door. The door creaks just a little and I turn to see if Nina has heard it. But she's still talking to Gage.

With this newfound bravery I have in me, I walk into my sister's room.

A chill runs up my spine. I can smell her. I inhale like I've run out of air and breath my sister in. A ball forms in my throat, something that hasn't happened in a long time, but no tears come out. I look up at her wall of leaves and my chest feels like it's going to cave in.

The front door slams and I hear my mom and dad yelling out for me. They sound angry. But I don't care.

"Mateo, where are you? Why did you make that video?" I hear my mom yelling from the living room.

When they can't find me, they show up in Lily's doorway. Nina comes out of her room and joins them. The anger on my parents faces seems to vanish in an instant when they look inside of Lily's room.

"Because I had to," I say. "I did it for Lily."

Instead of saying anything they come into Lily's room and take me into their arms. Nina rushes in and joins them. Soon we're all huddled on the ground holding each other. It stays like this for a while.

Later on after we talk about the video, I come back into Lily's room by myself and sit on her bed. The vigil is coming up and I'm more ready now than ever. My only hope is that the video will do something, maybe it will spark fire in other people. At least I hope so.

"Hey," someone whispers from the doorway. I turn and see Nina standing there, a smile on her face.

"Not tired?" I ask her and she comes into the room and sits down next to me.

"I am, I just wanted to check on you. You know Mom and Dad aren't really mad at you about the video. They are just trying to deal with everything in the best way possible. They don't want us getting hurt. They want something done just as much as we do." I'm still new to having full-on conversations with Nina, but this feels nice.

"I know," I tell her. "But I needed to do something. Paco is right, the system is horrible and I'm scared it won't be handled the right way. I want people to know her name. I want people to know her."

"Me too, which is why I'm glad you spoke up. I'm not sure I would've been able to." Nina shakes her head and looks down at her nails. "I'm not brave like that."

"Lily said we're already brave. We just need to find it in ourselves sometimes because it might be hiding like those raccoons that steal Coco's food on the back porch." I add a little joke in like Lily used to when she tried to explain something important to me. It made me laugh but it helped so much more.

Nina giggles and flicks me on the ear.

"You're a pain and goof, but you're cool, Mateo."

"I know," I smirk.

My eyes land on Lily's record player.

"Want to listen to Lily's favorite song with me?"
I ask Nina and she looks over at the record player, not
sure it's a good idea.

Instead of waiting for her to respond I get up,
close the door to Lily's bedroom, and walk over to the
player. Through the clear lid, I can see the David Bowie
record is still in there. I pull the headphones out from
under the table and put them over my head, letting the
thick black rubber suction to my ears. I give the other
pair to Nina. She puts them on and smiles at me.

For a moment I can hear my own heartbeat but
it's quickly cut off by me turning the player on. I skip
to *Heroes* and Nina and I lay down on Lily's carpet. I
stare up at her ceiling and notice she tacked a few
leaves around the light fixture. Nina turns to me and we
laugh. Lily's obsession with leaves and nature was

always something Nina joked about with her. I press the play button with the tip of my crutch and Lily's favorite song in the entire world starts.

The music flows through the headphones and instead of making me hurt, it makes me smile, and when I look over at Nina, I see it's done the same thing for her.

527 000 views. That's how many my video got. The media coverage is insane and even though my mom and dad are still a little worried, Mr. Curtis says that this is good. That this will help us a lot, but he's not making any promises. I didn't expect for the video to get this big, but I'm glad it did and so are Queenie and Marcus. This has become something more than we hoped and I can only hope that it does something for Lily's case and for any other victims of police brutality.

The vigil has turned into a rally and when we got to the library this morning, there were already news vans outside, some even from other cities. I just hope this helps Lily's case. I hope this shows the police department that we're not backing down. We'll never back down.

"How many people are out there?" my dad asks Mr. Curtis. He pulls my dad to the side and whispers in his ear. My dad's head jerks to the side and he looks at me, his eyes super wide.

"Mateo! Guess who's here?" Queenie comes out from behind a table of helpers where her dad is standing. He's been more help than I thought. I had no idea that Queenie's dad's girlfriend Megan helped with organizing rallies and marches. Now she's co-conducting this one with Queenie.

"Who?" I hurry up to her.

"Carmella Hollis is here! She's going to speak!" a huge smile forms on her face.

Fortunately, I happen to know who she is. She's running for President this year and has been all over the news. I seriously can't believe she's here.

"This is great, Queenie!" I say and my mom comes up to me and taps me on the shoulder.

"This is so big, Mateo. Lily would be so proud of you, mijo." Mom pulls me in and hugs me. "Your dad said there's a lot of people outside. Megan wants to know if you'd like to be the first to speak."

I look into my mom's tear-filled eyes. I don't need to think about it. I already know what I'm going to tell her.

"Yes," I tell my mom and hug her back.

I think about Lily and how I think she'd be proud of me too. I just wish I could see her one more time and see her smile again. But I know wherever she is she's smiling at me, probably flicking my ears, even though I don't feel it. A smile grows on my face and I turn to my mom and dad.

"It's almost time," Queenie says from behind me. I turn to her and yank her into a hug.

"Thank you so much, Queenie. I know Lily would've loved this," I tell Queenie and she hugs me back and starts to cry. It feels like forever before we let each other go.

"Hey," Marcus calls from the other end of the building. He just got here and I'm glad his mom let him come to this. That smile on his face sends warm vibes through me and I happen to know he feels the same way.

Marcus walks up to me and without saying a word I hug him. He laughs and the hugs me back super tight. I don't know how I would've got through all of this without him. A part of me feels like Lily sent him to me and I think I'd like to keep it that way.

"Thank you," is all I say to him. He whispers back that he'll always be here for me and my heart flutters in my chest.

"It's time!" Megan calls out to us. I let go of Marcus and he follows Queenie back to the table to help with posters and pins.

I look down at my pin that reads JUSTICE FOR LILY and flick it like she used to flick my ears. *This is all for you,* I say in my head and I hope she can hear it.

Nina comes out from the restroom, her makeup a bit messy. We walk over to our mom and dad and I get in the middle. I nod to Megan and Queenie by the door and Mr. Curtis opens the double doors of the library for us. I can see flashes from cameras going off and a nervous flutter comes to life in me.

"Ready?" my dad asks me, my mom, and Nina.

We all nod at him.

As a family, we walk out the double doors and into the afternoon light. Camera flashes blind me for a second but then I can see what's really going on. My eyes fly wide open and for a moment I feel like can't breathe. There are hundreds of people in front of the library and even more filling the entire street. People are holding signs with Lily's face on them and they are chanting *Justice For Lily.*

Something builds inside of me like when you fill a water balloon and are afraid it will bust. My sister's smile on a poster catches my eye and then all at once, everything rushes out, the sadness, the pain, the tears.

The tears flood my eyes and create streaks of sorrow down my cheeks. I don't care that it took me so long to cry, I don't care that I was scared to feel anything. All I care about in this single moment, is that smile on Lily's face.

Maybe Mr. Curtis and Megan are right. Maybe this will help Lily out more than we hoped. The fact that so many people cared enough about Lily to show up makes me so incredibly happy. I want to thank and hug every single one of them. They didn't even know my sister but here they are for her. It doesn't matter if they didn't know her. I will help them get to know my sister, I will help them know Lily.

1 YEAR LATER

Lily never did get the justice she deserved.

But I fought so hard for her and so did my friends, my family, our entire community, and so many other people around the world. Officer Woods didn't get charged with Lily's death. He left town a few months after because no one looks at you the same after you kill somebody, especially somebody like Lily.

But even though we couldn't get justice for Lily, I will still hold on to my voice and still use it for others who can't. I'm not done and I never will be. As long as people continue to go through what my family and I did, I will be right behind them, fighting for the stolen ones.

Things are going to get much harder, but I know Lily is still there, watching over me and laughing at me when I sing along to David Bowie in the mirror.

"*Bravery isn't a hard thing to find in yourself...*" Lily had once said. She was right about bravery. When you do find it in yourself, it is truly the best feeling ever and when you use it for good, it can light up the world and give hope to people who've lost it, which is exactly what I'm going to do.

I'm going to help everyone be brave. Brave like me. *Brave Like Lily.*

RICHARD CARDENAS resides in El Paso, Texas. He enjoys reading, pizza, horror movies, and making videos on his YouTube channel.

CPSIA information can be obtained
at www.ICGtesting.com
Printed in the USA
LVHW052142040719
623151LV00013B/452